DAUGHTERS OF IRAQ

Revital Shiri-Horowitz

ISBN-13: 978-0-6154607-9-6

Translation: Shira Atik
Editing: Abe Brennan
Photography and cover design: Vered Mizrahi

*Dedicated with love to the women in
my family, and to women all over
the world whose voices are silenced.*

Contents:

Chapter One: Violet Rosen

Monday, October 15, 1986

Baghdad 1940

"**V**iolet! Violet Twaina!" *Aba's* voice thundered. "Come here this instant!"

"My father's calling me," I said to my best friend, Naima. "Don't go anywhere. I'll be right back." I ran up the narrow stairway that led to my family's house. When I looked into *Aba's* eyes, I knew I was in serious trouble. My heart froze.

"Violet Twaina!" My father stood fuming, rocking on his heels, hands buried deep inside his pockets. "Mrs. Chanukah called from school. She said you talked back to Mrs. Zbeida today." The terrifying glare accompanying his words seemed a sure sign harsh punishment awaited me.

"What are you talking about? I didn't do anything," I said, crossing my fingers behind my back, desperate to wheedle out of the situation.

"Don't tell me stories, Violet," my father said. "I know you're lying, and I know you talked back! Mrs. Chanukah doesn't call parents out of the blue and waste their precious time. She said Mrs. Zbeida asked you to stop talking, and you told her you hadn't been talking, that maybe it was time for her to get her hearing checked once and for all, because this wasn't the first time she'd blamed you for something you hadn't done."

"That's not true. That's not how it happened! She's always accusing me of things I didn't do. I hate that teacher," I said. "She picks on me for no reason. She's very rude to me. She told me to shut up, but I wasn't even talking. And," I continued, unable to stop myself, "I said it very politely. All I said is that she must have misheard, because it wasn't me. If you want, you can ask Naima," I said, dragging my poor friend into my scheme.

"Go tell Naima to come upstairs right away." My father's voice was angry; I could tell he didn't believe me. I went down and called Naima, trying to think of how I could buy her cooperation.

"Naima," I said. "My father wants to ask you something, and you really have to help me. If you do what I tell you, I'll give you Fahima as a present." Fahima was my most beautiful doll. She had long flowing hair I loved to comb and several outfits my mother had sewn especially for her.

"Fahima?" Naima asked. "If I do what you say, you'll really give me Fahima?"

"Yes, I swear, I'll give her to you." I raised my hands to my heart and looked right into her eyes. I knew she wouldn't be able to resist. "That vicious teacher Mrs. Zbeida, she's always getting me into trouble. You have to tell my father I didn't say a thing in school today. Tell him everything I told him is true."

"*Wai li*," said Naima, grinning. "The way you spoke to her! The whole class was rolling on the floor."

"*Ya'allah*," I said. "I promise I'll give you Fahima, alright? What's the big deal?"

8

"Okay, fine, I'll do it," she said. "But what if your father finds out we're lying?"

She had reason to be worried, but my style was to jump into icy water first, then think about it later. "I don't know. Let's not think about it. Come on, he's waiting for us."

We went upstairs. *Aba* sat in the living room, in a big red armchair covered in an embroidered fabric flecked with real gold. When we walked into the room, he turned a menacing gaze on us. Normally my father would have asked after Naima's family, but he got straight to the point.

"I understand something happened in school today," he said.

Naima stared at the floor. "Yes," she said. "Yes, Mr. Twaina. A lot of things happened in school today. Which one do you mean?"

"I understand that Mrs. Zbeida got angry at Violet during class. Can you tell me what happened?"

Naima tried to fulfill her part of the deal. In a voice not much louder than a whisper, she said, "Mrs. Zbeida didn't get angry at Violet at all."

I hadn't thought of this. My father had outsmarted me; instead of offering my story for her verification, he had allowed Naima to make up her own version.

"That's not what Mrs. Chanukah told me!" he hissed.

"Mr. Twaina," Naima said, "Violet is such a good student, so quiet and serious. Nobody could ever complain about her. She sits so nicely in class. She pays attention, she doesn't talk, and she always does her homework. It doesn't seem possible she did anything wrong. Mrs. Chanukah must have gotten her mixed up with this other girl who's always bothering her and called you instead of the other parents."

Even I could tell she had gone too far. And *Aba*— who knew me very well, who knew I could never be the angelic little girl Naima described—couldn't decide whether to laugh or cry. Realizing Naima would be of no help, he called for his driver and sent her home. I knew exactly what would happen next. *This is it*, I thought. *I'm doomed*. A week under "house arrest." No going out to see people, nobody coming to see me. As for the beating, I wasn't afraid. Whenever my father hit me, I imagined my nephew Eddie, my sister Farida, and I jumping into the river, and all I was feeling was the touch of water on my skin.

My father didn't yell. He glared at me and said, "I know you, and I know that you talked back to your teacher. Not only did you lie to me, but you made Naima lie to me as well. You are a bad girl. You have no respect for anyone, and you don't care about anything. The only one you care about is yourself. Well, I'll show you exactly what you are. Go to my closet and bring me my thickest belt. Go on. I'll wait for you right here. If you try to trick me by bringing a different belt, I'll beat you with both of them."

I went to my parents' room. Nothing could help me now. The other children of the family saw me crying, but they didn't say a word; they were already used to these scenes. I was the only girl in my family consistently beaten, and everyone knew why. I was the rebellious child. I dodged responsibilities, and I pushed limits. I wasn't afraid of anything, and I did whatever I wanted. I lied constantly, with no remorse. I ran away to the river with Eddie, I talked back to the teachers, I skipped classes, and I stole money from mother's drawer for candy. In other words, I knew how to live, and I didn't let any person, or any consequence, dampen my adventurous spirit.

My father beat me that day—he beat me whenever I did anything stupid—but his anger drove him beyond a normal thrashing, and my mother was forced to intercede. She pleaded with him to stop, and finally he did. My back hurt, my bottom hurt, and I couldn't move. And of course he told me that until Eddie's Bar Mitzvah, which was ten days away, I could only leave the house for school, and I had to come straight home. I couldn't play outside, and I couldn't see my friends. *Aba's* driver would take me to school in the morning and bring me home in the afternoon. None of this broke my spirit, though, because I knew a little patience was all I needed; then I could go back to doing as I pleased. I never gave Fahima to Naima. I told her she hadn't lived up to her end of the bargain and that she'd gotten me into even more trouble. Back then, that was how I behaved.

Chapter Two: Farida Sasson

Farida felt uneasy about doing her usual Sunday errands. She had both a daily routine and a weekly routine, and she tried to stick to them; she knew if she fell behind, the pressure would be too much for her. Sunday was supposed to be haircut day. After spending all day Friday cooking, by the next morning she usually looked haggard, and her fine hair was imbued with kitchen smells. On that particular Sunday morning, however, she was reluctant to leave the house for her weekly salon visit. The heat was oppressive, and newscasters talked of terrorist attacks. In order to reach her appointment, she would have to wait for the 15 Bus which came only once an hour take the bus to the center of town, and then walk to Shimon's Salon, situated next door to Chaim the Moroccan's butcher, right below the new Chinese restaurant. Because of all the talk about bombs, Farida didn't want to take the bus, and so after much deliberation she decided to stay home and cook okra patties for her grandchildren, who were visiting the following day.

She rinsed the okra, removed the stalks, sliced an onion and sautéed it. While she worked, her thoughts drifted to Baghdad, the city of her birth. Farida remembered the large houses with the enormous courtyards, designed to accommodate prodigious families like hers. Each wing of her house was inhabited by a different family: *Aba, Ima,* Violet, and Farida herself, the youngest daughter, lived in one wing; her sister

Farcha, along with her husband Sammy and their three children, lived in another; her brother Anwar lived in a third wing with his wife Yasmin and their three daughters; in yet another wing, her sister Habiba lived with her husband Yaakov and their five impish kids. Farida loved her nieces and nephews as if they were her own siblings, perhaps because they were closer to her age than her own brothers and sisters. She and Violet were the youngest of the brood. Georgia, their mother, had given birth to Habiba, Farcha, and Anwar at a very young age. She then had two more children, both of whom died in infancy. After many years, the two girls were born less than two years apart, brightening Georgia's heart and bringing her solace. By the time Farida and Violet were born, they were aunts to Edward, Habiba and Yaakov's oldest son. The rest of the nieces and nephews came later. Eddie as he was called by everyone, was born one year before Violet, and a year and a half after Violet was born, Farida came into the world.

Farida remembered how she, Eddie, and Violet used to sneak out of school. They would look for a horse-drawn carriage, jump on its back, and hitch rides through the streets of Baghdad. If the driver caught sight of the kids, he beat them with his horsewhip and cursed them for not paying the fare. Later, when they were a little older, they raced to nearby Chidekel River, took off their clothes, and swam in its cool waters, free from trouble and pain, splashing each other and laughing endlessly.

During summer, when Baghdad's rivers dried up, tiny islands surfaced—*jazira*, they were called—and the children searched them for water creatures. They'd pick up animals and insects and examine them. Then they'd dress, pack up, and return home, pretending to come straight from school. Because they went to the Jewish school, the teachers knew all the parents, and if the instructors ever suspected anything, they dropped in for unannounced visits. The kids knew that when a teacher came to the house, their punishment would be severe. They paid the price for their adventures willingly, taking comfort in knowing they would return, again and again, to these moments of pure delight.

"Ach," Farida sighed. "It's a shame, *walla*, it is such a shame." She was talking to herself in the empty kitchen. "It's a shame we couldn't have had that kind of life together." Farida and Eddie had shared a special closeness during childhood, which later blossomed into a full-fledged love. Farida's heart clenched at the thought that she and Eddie couldn't get married, couldn't bring children into the world. "He was so handsome . . ." She sighed again. "And his eyes, don't get me started, those eyes . . ." She continued to ruminate, first aloud, then silently, remembering different episodes from her life, scenes that made her feel his absence, and his loss, more acutely than ever.

She sliced the okra, and the vegetable's color made her think of his green eyes, the intelligence she saw there. Tears slid down her cheeks. She wiped them with the edge of her sleeve to keep them from dripping onto the okra and put down the knife. For a long time she stood, stooped over the cutting board, until the wave of emotions had passed; then she straightened, took another stalk from the platter on the counter, scraped its rough edges, and returned it to the platter. After preparing the vegetables, she dipped her hands in water and began composing the filling for the *kubot*—the semolina pockets. She took ground chicken mixed with parsley and spices, placed it on the dough, and rolled the mixture into small balls, which she dropped into a steaming pot of water.

Farida thought of mid-1940s Iraq. She remembered how Yasmin, Anwar's wife, had finally given him a son after three daughters, how they celebrated his birth with a *chalri*—a traditional Arabian party with belly-dancing. The *chalri* took place on the seventh day after the child's birth—the day before his *brit*. Farida's parents invited relatives from all across Baghdad, Hilla, and Basra. All the important people in the Jewish community were invited. Farida's mother, Georgia, was a pillar of Baghdad's Jewry; she came from a family of well-known rabbis, and it was a great honor to attend one of her parties. The family overlooked nothing: the best musicians and singers were summoned to the *chalri*, along with a famous belly dancer who strutted before wild-eyed spectators. Some men stuck bills into her belt and bra, and everyone sang and danced and showered the new baby and his family with blessings.

After the birth of her son, Yasmin took to her bed and barely rose for forty days. At that stage, her duty was to take care of the new baby and to rest. The women from her extended family waited upon and fed her, tended to her and her baby's needs. It was traditional for female relatives to care for the mother, house, other children (if there were any), and the husband, so that a mother could regain her strength and resume ministering to her family. The women did this with great joy and unlimited generosity.

That was a good year: it featured a charmed birth as well as Eddie's Bar Mitzvah. He was the first grandson of the family and everyone's darling. And despite the fact he was almost thirteen, and she was not yet ten, and notwithstanding that this was often when families separated related boys and girls because of the new, strange, amorphous tension between them, Farida remembered they couldn't stand being apart, not even for a day. Whenever they saw each other, they secretly pledged their love for each other until the end of time.

On the day of Yasmin's baby's birth, Eddie, Violet, and Farida were given an important task: they were sent to tell all their acquaintances about the child. Once word got out, the women—relatives, servants, Arab and Jewish neighbors alike—began to trill loudly, celebrating the happy event. Those who hadn't yet heard the news now understood: something wonderful had occurred in the Twaina household.

At the conclusion of that festive day, the merry trio split up as usual and returned to sleep in their separate homes. It was a stifling Baghdadi night. In the height of summer, when it was too hot to sleep in their beds, people camped on roofs. Farida and Violet, along with their parents, slept atop one of the wings of the big house, while Eddie and his family reposed above another wing. After the excitement of the day, Eddie, Violet, and Farida had trouble falling asleep; they gazed at the lovely full moon shining in the distant sky, at innumerable stars. They were filled with a sense of great satisfaction and indescribable joy. A new son had been born into the family, and they were all part of this creation.

Chapter Three: Noa Rosen

Noa rushed from the apartment. She hadn't heard the alarm go off. She'd awakened in a fog to discover it was 8:20. In less than an hour, her *Introduction to Jewish Philosophy* exam would start; it was an important test, and she'd been studying for days. She'd writhed most the night, sleepless, and when she finally did nod off, she'd had a bizarre dream. The course material morphed with her daily life. Angels moved between spheres, changed levels, revealed different faces, gathered around her. *Michael and Gabriel,* she thought. Her brother Guy appeared, but as a small boy with angel wings on his back. Her mother Violet was in it, too. She wrapped Noa in her arms, and Noa felt wonderfully safe. She told her mother she missed her very much and was so happy she'd finally come home. Her mother's hair had grown back; she'd worn a wig the last time they'd seen each other. But when she reached for her mother's head, the hair became the kabbalistic chart she'd memorized the previous night. The alarm screeched, and she woke, trembling.

Sitting on the bus, bleary-eyed, she tried interpreting the dream. Angels going up and down, and *Ima,* and Guy . . . no wonder she'd woken up wearier than she'd been the night before. A multitude of thoughts scrolled through her mind, and she attempted to make sense of them. This was Noa's second year of studying Hebrew literature. She supported herself by working in the university library. She believed in financial independence and refused to be a full-time student unless she could pay her own tuition and living costs.

After her mother died, Noa had extended her tour of duty in the army. She needed the stability and was happy to be far from home. When she completed her military service as a lieutenant, she began saving for college and decided to see a bit of the world. She worked as a waitress, then traveled with Barak, her former boyfriend. When she attended university, she assumed a heavy course load and worked in the library as many hours as she could.

Noa had never believed her strong, vigorous mother would succumb to the cancer that struck when Noa was fourteen. Violet's stubbornness had bought her a few more years in the bosom of her family, but Noa, like most teenagers, was absorbed in her own life. She didn't understand how little time her mother had left, so she hadn't spent the last days at Violet's bedside.

One fall morning, as Violet underwent a round of chemotherapy, all the systems in her body failed. Noa received a summons in the midst of her tour, and Guy was called out of school. Violet never regained consciousness, and she died the same night, leaving her husband and children broken and aching. Noa was twenty.

The bus was crammed with university students, teenagers, and old people. Noa rested her nose and forehead against the frame of the open window. Though only June, the hot mornings had become oppressive. People pushed up against one another, and the smells of sweat, spices, and fresh vegetables from the market blended into a pungent odor. Noa didn't notice the chaos. She was in her head, floating to other destinations. The smell of spices and fresh vegetables conjured Aunt Farida, her mother's sister. She heard Farida's husky voice—a testament to many years of cigarette smoking. It was soothing and brought a faint smile to Noa's lips. Noa saw her aunt's stout body, heard the heavy Iraqi accent. Farida was Noa's favorite aunt: a tender woman in a large, awkward body.

Farida was truly an enormous woman: her breasts sagged upon her gargantuan belly and grazed her hips. Noa yearned for her aunt's warm touch, which had quietly protected her over the years. Aunt Farida's demeanor was kind and reassuring: her nose was as wide as her heart, and her forehead was plowed with wrinkles, which vanished when she smiled. She had a large chin with a dimple in the middle and dark, sympathetic eyes that always looked tired. Aunt Farida's life had not been easy, but despite the hardships, she exuded optimism and love. Like a Bozo the Clown punching bag, when she went down, she popped right back up. She was always so encouraging, a safe haven in Noa's turbulent life. Noa didn't like to think about what she would have done without her.

Noa continued deciphering her strange dream. She understood it had something to do with the exam, but she couldn't remember the obscure words her brother had whispered. She searched for a connection between the dream and her current preoccupations and thoughts.

Her mind returned to her mother, and her eyes teared up when she imagined sharing her thoughts and struggles with Violet. Noa yearned for the comforts of a real home. Her childhood house was nothing like it had been before her mother died; in fact, it was barely recognizable. Every inch of the house, it seemed, was steeped in sadness. The joy that once filled the home, that had almost burst through its walls, had disappeared; now it reminded her of a deserted, queenless castle on the verge of collapse. The study, once packed with papers, had been abandoned; the fragrance of spices was gone, too. And Noa's grandfather had immersed himself in his own affairs. Since the death of his wife, Georgia, he had buried himself both in work and, in the last two years, his studies. He made a point of cooking dinner every Friday night in an attempt to maintain the family's long-time tradition of eating together once a week. But the meals weren't the same without Violet.

Noa wanted to fall into Farida's arms, rest there, recuperate. Maybe she'd visit her after the test. She had no plans for the rest of the day, and the test would only take three hours. If she caught the noon bus, she'd reach the village within two hours. Yes, that's what she would do. She'd call Aunt Farida and ask what was for supper. She'd board the bus, wind through the streets to her aunt's house. She recalled the smells of familiar and beloved Iraqi dishes. Aunt Farida would spoil her: feed her and send her home with packages of food for the rest of the week. Yes, she'd call her after the test. Noa remembered other times arriving at Aunt Farida's house, forlorn, defiant, like a rebellious teenager. Farida always smiled, plied her with pots of good food and luscious pastries—all the comforts of a real home.

Noa emerged from her daydream. She hadn't noticed the bus moving or the passengers getting on and off. She had no memory of traversing the usual route from her apartment on the Street of the Prophets to the gates of the university. She almost forgot to disembark near the Gilman building, where the test would be given. While entering the building she slammed her leg into the security guard's table and stifled a scream. She plodded up the stairs, one step at a time. Only when she sat down for the exam did she feel her distracted mind focus. The morning daydreams receded. Noa bent over the paper, concentrating on her mission. She took a deep breath, rotated her head, shook out her arms, stretched her muscles. Everything had been leading up to this test. She had studied day and night, imbibed the material. She was like a trained soldier ready for battle. Wasn't she?

Noa lifted her head and looked around. She saw the heads of the other students bent over their work. She looked at the preceptor. The woman walked past her, offered a candy, and wished her luck, like she could read the doubt in her mind. She could do this, Noa thought. If she just relaxed a little, the lines of text would stop dancing before her. Noa took more deep breaths and again looked at the test. She read the first question, then the next four, and she knew her hard work had paid off. She began to write.

Chapter Four: At Aunt Farida's

"Hello, my sweet girl, my soul, may God bless you, how did you know I was thinking about you all morning?" Farida hugged Noa and planted wet kisses on both cheeks. "I missed you—what were you thinking: why didn't you call me all week?"

"Hi, Aunt Farida," Noa said, leaning into her aunt's soft, warm body, wrapping her arms around her, absorbing warmth and security. "I was so busy—you know how it is. Work, school, exams . . . even today I had an exam. You see? I came to visit as soon as I could. What's that fantastic smell? Okra?" She headed for the kitchen, following the scent.

"You've always had a sharp sense of smell, a blessing on your head. I'm so glad you came—there's okra with meat dumplings, just what you like, and as you can see, I'm also making *machbuz*," she said, tempting her niece with the promise of Noa's favorite Iraqi pastries. "Eat, eat," urged Farida, taking a tray out of the oven, "and when you go, I'll send you home with a bag of Purim goodies." She laughed. "Now tell me, Noa, how was the test?"

"It was fine." Noa let out a loud sigh, popping a piece of cheese pastry into her mouth. "I'm glad it's over. This exam was weighing on me. There was so much material, you can't even imagine. I spent so much time at my desk my behind was starting to ache . . ."

"*Nu*, I'm sure you did well. With your mother's intelligence and your father's good looks, you'll go far," Farida said, clasping her hands.

Noa laughed. "Wait a minute, what are you saying? That my mother was ugly and my father stupid?"

"God forbid!" Farida said, wringing her hands, spitting, doing whatever she could to disperse any evil spirits lingering outside her door. "Your mother, *allah yirchama(may god bless her memory)*, was beautiful *and* good *and* smart, and your father—is there anything that man can't do? *Ya'allah*, come here and sit down." Farida pointed to the empty chair across from her. "When you've finished eating, we'll get to work. You see," she said with a smile, "I already made the dough for the *machbuz*."

"I came at the right time," Noa said, laughing. "As if you really need help. . . but, actually, I'm in the mood to bake something together." Noa leaned back. "Do you remember when I was little, I would spend my vacations with you, and Sigali and I would help you bake? We each had our own little jobs: Sigali was in charge of rolling the date spread into little balls and stuffing them into the dough, and my job was to dip the dough in water and sprinkle it with sesame seeds."

"Yes, of course I remember, that's what's called '*Tena Maca*.'" Farida's laugh disintegrated into a coughing fit, and she cursed her cigarettes.

"*Tena Maca*? What's that?"

"Ah," Farida sighed. "*Tena Maca* is a code word for babysitting. If a woman needed a little peace and quiet, she would ask her neighbor to give her children a *Tena Maca*—to keep them occupied for a few minutes . . . Oh, baking was such a *Tena Maca*." She waved her hand.

"You and Sigali helped me in the kitchen, and Uncle Moshe got to rest a little bit. *Ya'allah*, my sweet girl, even though Uncle Moshe's been gone awhile, and nobody in this house needs a *Tena Maca*, I'll still let you help me. But first, have a drink, taste my okra—I even have some rice ready. Work can wait a bit."

Farida scanned her niece from head to toe. "What's the matter, Noa'le? You don't look good to me today." She piled fresh-baked treats onto Noa's plate. "What? You're not sleeping at night? You've lost a little weight. What's going on? Aren't you eating?"

"No, Aunt Farida, really, I'm fine. And what's this about losing weight? I wish." Noa gave her aunt a rueful smile. "Actually, it wouldn't be so bad if I lost a few pounds. It's this test," she added. "I didn't sleep well last night." Noa sat next to the little table. It was loaded with delicacies, as if Farida were planning to feed an entire platoon. "Is someone else coming?"

"No," Aunt Farida said, a little sadly.

"So who are you cooking for?"

Aunt Farida sat in the chair opposite her, looked around, and sighed. "I don't know how to cook for two people. Only for an army—that's how it is. It's not so bad; whatever's left over, you can take back to your apartment." She gazed out the little kitchen window.

Children played outside, and the laughter made Farida forlorn. She remembered other days. For a moment there was a strained silence between the two women. Each seemed to be remembering: a house buoyant with life, crammed with people. So much had changed in recent years, leaving both of them yearning for the past.

Of Farida's children, Sigali had married and left the house first; then Oren got married. Sigali had two children before leaving her husband. "It killed me," she had said, "that he wasn't doing anything with his life." Oren lived in Nahariya and rarely visited. Sigali lived near Aunt Farida, and whenever one of her kids got sick, she brought the child over. But most of the time Sigali was busy with her own affairs; she was a single mother, and it wasn't easy. And Uncle Moshe . . . Uncle Moshe had died two years ago. Only Farida remained, and being alone was not easy for her.

For many years, Uncle Moshe was out of work, and the family lived off social security. Moshe suffered from what we call shell shock. He had left for war as a confident man and returned shattered, unable to transcend the trauma. From conversation fragments gleaned over years, Noa collected an assortment of images, and from those images she pieced together the complete story.

Uncle Moshe had fought in Sinai. He was the platoon's cook, and one morning he woke from a dreadful dream, soaked in sweat. In his dream, all the men in his unit were killed in a surprise attack by the Egyptians. Uncle Moshe had just climbed out of his sleeping bag and was looking for a quiet spot to urinate and calm his nerves when the bombing started. His friends didn't even make it out of their sleeping bags;

only Uncle Moshe found shelter, and he was saved. When it was all over, he realized his nightmare had become a horrific reality.

Uncle Moshe's life, and the lives of everyone in his family, would never be the same after the Yom Kippur War. He couldn't hold a job. Some nights he screamed and cried in his sleep; other nights he couldn't sleep at all. Aunt Farida loved her family fiercely and strove to maintain a sense of normalcy for Uncle Moshe and their kids. She ministered to him, and made sure his children respected him. Two years ago, Uncle Moshe's heart could no longer carry the burden of all those memories, and he died. Farida was left alone.

"*Ya'allah*, Noa, start eating," Farida urged. "The food is getting cold, and you haven't even touched it. Eat already, before it cools and becomes *jifa*—nobody wants rotten food. Now, tell your Aunt Farida a little about Noa: how is she doing, and when will she get married already, with God's help?"

"Really, Aunt Farida," Noa said, her mouth full. "Get married? Who exactly do you suggest I marry? I don't even have a serious boyfriend. You know Barak and I broke up."

"Do I know? Of course I know. Okay, I'll tell you the truth. You want the truth?" Farida hoped Noa would be willing to listen to her. Farida had a strong opinion on the issue—she had strong opinions on every issue—and it was hard to keep her thoughts to herself.

"Sure, I want the truth—why not?" Noa said, laying her fork on her plate. She knew nothing would keep her aunt from voicing her thoughts about Barak. She looked at her and waited.

"He's all wrong for you," Farida said with a dismissive wave of her hand. "He loves himself too much, what can I tell you? You need someone who loves you more than he loves himself. This young man is killing you."

"Right." Noa smiled. There was no ambiguity in Aunt Farida's outlook on the world; there was right, and there was wrong. "In the meantime, I'm kissing a lot of frogs," she said with a wink, "until I find a real prince."

"I pity those boys when you're around," Farida laughed. "Do they know they're just frogs in your eyes?" Her plump arms fell to her sides. "So some day, one of these frogs will turn into a prince? I like that idea. Now that I think about it, most of the men I've known were frogs, too. A couple were princes, including your father, God protect him. Do you know I saw him yesterday at Uncle Anwar's house? He is a good man, your father. I hear he's taking a class in geography, and sometimes you two meet between classes?"

"That's true," Noa said. She picked up her fork and took a bite, surprised and relieved the Barak conversation was over. "We do meet from time to time, and it's great we have new topics to discuss. He's quite the student," she said. "He never misses a lecture. You won't believe his latest kick: he wants to earn a doctorate in geography—*Ima's* field—and complete her research."

"Are you serious? I had no idea. Good for him," Farida said.

"You know, it's really nice to see him there," Noa said. "He's smiling again. He looks much younger."

"Good," Farida said, "very good. I'm happy for him. It's time he started looking for a wife, don't you think?" She grinned.

"It is time, but you know how it is. At that age, it's not so simple."

"Tell me about it!" Farida said. "I'm in the same predicament."

Noa felt uncomfortable. It would be difficult seeing her father with another woman. "So what's new with you, Aunt Farida?" Noa looked at her aunt's large hands. "Look how rude I'm being, I haven't even complimented you on your delicious okra. The crust is amazing. *Gute, gute*, like my grandmother would say. Just how I like it. We've been talking about me this whole time. What's going on in your life? How are Sigali and the kids? I haven't seen them in ages."

"Bless God's name forever and ever, may his name be blessed, I can't complain," Farida said, staring at the kitchen ceiling and shaking her hands toward heaven. "Look, I'm keeping busy, as you can see. I couldn't even make it to the hairdresser, and tomorrow Sigali's taking half a day's vacation and bringing the kids for a visit. Can you believe that Ruthie's in second grade already? You should see this little slip of a girl reading and writing like the devil. And Shai is in his last year of preschool, driving his teacher crazy. Did you know he has a male teacher this year?"

"What? A man teaching preschool?"

"That's right. You don't need breasts to enter the profession anymore. He's a fantastic teacher," Farida said. "He takes the kids on nature walks, teaches them plant names. He knows all the songs, and on *Pesach* (Passover) he taught the kids how to stomp grapes and make wine."

"Nice," Noa said, impressed.

"But while we're on the subject of me," Farida said, "it's not easy living alone. The days are one thing, I keep busy, but the nights . . ." She tried to recline, but her corpulent body slid forward on the seat, and she couldn't get comfortable.

"I can't fall asleep at night," said Farida. "The nights go on forever—they have a beginning, but no end. I go to bed as late as I can, I watch the late shows, and I still can't fall asleep. I wander the house like a sleepwalker. I have no idea what's going on . . . maybe it's my age or the approach of summer . . . maybe it's the heat." She looked at Noa's plate. "You ate everything, a blessing on your head—come, let's clean up and start baking."

Aunt Farida stood and walked to the counter, which was covered with delicious food. She bent to pick up the huge platter that sat beside the neat rows of spices; her house dress rose, reavealing a pair of thick legs. She rummaged around one of the shelves for the baking implements she'd had for so many years. After clearing the table, Farida put down the yeasty dough that had already risen. Taking pleasure in its appearance, in its very presence, she rolled it into a log and split it into two pieces, one of which she gave to Noa. The two women, one young, one old, sat by the table and rolled the dough into tiny balls. They were making *sambusak bejiben,* a cheese-filled pastry. Later, they'd fill some of the dough with dates and sprinkle it with sesame seeds. The sweet smell of these yeast cookies, or *baba,* would fill the room. The women fell silent as they concentrated on their tasks. Both focused on their own work, engrossed in their own thoughts.

"From everything you're telling me," Noa said, returning to the topic of Farida's sleeplessness, "it sounds serious. Maybe you should try warm milk. Or deep breathing, like they do in yoga."

"Nothing's going to help," Farida said, "it's awful. *Ya'allah,* forget it. There's no point in discussing it."

"Well, if we're pouring our hearts out," Noa said. "If we're talking about truth and feelings . . ." She spoke slowly, eyes averted, concentrating on her work, as if rolling little balls of dough was the most important thing she'd ever done. "I've been very unhappy lately. I don't know what's going on."

"As soon as I saw your face in the doorway I knew something wasn't right," Farida said. She raised her arms, then put her hands to her cheeks and shook her head from side to side. "My girl, a blessing on your head, why are you sad? What's missing in your life? Maybe you should live with your father again? Maybe leaving home wasn't such a good idea? You had everything you could ask for living there. And now you've left your father all alone. I've been saying for a long time that living by yourself in that apartment was a mistake." She wagged her finger. "If you lived at home, your father could take care of you. He could cook and do your laundry. What's so great about all this solitude, anyway?"

"Maybe, Aunt Farida. I've thought about it; we'll see." Noa was losing patience. She hadn't come to be lectured, and she certainly hadn't meant to upset her aunt. She drew a deep breath. "It's not as simple as you think. I miss *Ima* so much—every day I long for her more," she said, eyes on the table. "I'm asking myself questions, and I'm not getting answers. Do you understand?" Noa finally lifted her head, searching her aunt's face. "I keep asking myself, where is she when I need her? I know it makes no sense."

"Not everything in life makes sense, Noa'le," Aunt Farida said. "It is what it is, as the young people say," she added, half smiling.

"But do you understand? I feel like she disappeared too soon, like I don't know enough about her, her family, you, your childhood. *Ima* didn't talk about growing up. And I have my own feelings of guilt," Noa said, pointing to her heart. "I feel like maybe I wasn't there for her when she needed me." Her voice was soft, and she spoke fast, as if worried she wouldn't be able to speak if she slowed down.

"What? Why are you tormenting yourself?" This conversation was hard for Farida, and she distracted herself by putting all her energy into rolling the dough into little balls. "You were in the army when your mother got sick. What could you have done?"

"It's true. I was in the army." Noa looked her aunt in the face. She took a deep breath and forced herself to examine the whole truth, all at once. *Let it all out*, she told herself. *Don't keep anything inside your aching heart; tell Aunt Farida the whole thing before she has a chance to stop you.* "I was in the army, but I was selfish. I should have asked to serve closer to home, but instead I ran away, ran from the sickness. I couldn't stand watching her body deteriorate. Her beautiful face looked more and more sunken every time I saw her, like her eyes were about to meet, like her cheeks were stuck together. I couldn't abide her trying to convince me everything was fine, that she was strong. I knew there was no chance she'd make it. It was just a matter of time. I can't live with these thoughts all the time, do you understand?" Tears streamed down her cheeks, and her breathing grew ragged.

"Do you understand?" Noa caught her breath. "I wanted to get used to her absence before she was even gone. I tried to see what it was like to live without her, and the whole time I knew that when it got to be too much, I'd have a place to go, and she'd always welcome me with a smile. I didn't think about *her*," she said, bowing her head. "I didn't think about how hard it was for her, don't you see?" I only thought about myself," she said again, pointing her index finger at herself, jabbing it into her ribs. "I never thought about how I wasn't there for her on a daily basis. I withdrew while she was still with us, and I didn't take advantage of the time we had left. And for that I can never forgive myself."

"Oh, my child," Aunt Farida said, taking Noa's hands in her own. "Now listen—listen very closely. Your mother was glad you were busy, that you had a full and productive life, and that you were a successful army officer. At first she was sad when you enlisted, but when she saw how good it was for you, she was happy. And when you became the first officer in our family, she was so proud. She talked about it all the time. The truth is, she was relieved you didn't see her suffer. She wanted to shield you from her pain; she knew how hard her illness was on you. Your mother talked about you all the time, told me everything you told her, every detail. And to every detail, she piled on her own blessings. Your mother didn't expect you, a girl of nineteen, to sit with her all day and watch her suffer. You're a kind and sensitive soul, Noa'le; your mother would have been just as proud of you today. It's good that you think about her, that you miss her. It's good, my girl. But sadness?" She stroked Noa's face. "What a waste," she said. "Really, that's no good. Oh, the pastries are burning." She shuffled over to the oven to take out the dessert, which was truly on the verge of ruin.

Noa tried to digest what she'd been told. There were so many things she hadn't known. She'd never realized her mother had understood her, that she hadn't been angry with her. She was struck by how much she didn't know about her mother.

Aunt Farida stood behind Noa and stroked her long hair. "Shhh . . . shhh . . . it's alright," she whispered. "Everything's alright, my child, my dear one. It's good that you told me all these things. It's good to cry, to release it all. You know I'm always here for you, my darling, no matter what . . . How did we get to the point of tears? You must have been thinking about these things for a long time."

Aunt Farida walked around and stood in front of Noa. Her voice was gentle. "Now listen very carefully to what I'm about to tell you. You're a big girl. You're independent. You're everything your mother wanted you to be, from the time you were in the womb. She wanted a girl exactly like you: sensitive, smart, thoughtful, loving. Even when you were little, you made your mother so proud. And I know your mother, of blessed memory, is looking down now and marveling at what a good job she did raising you. You're an adult. You're strong." She spoke slowly. "And for that reason, for that very reason . . ." She paused, considering her words. "It's for that reason I can now give you something I couldn't give you before."

"What is it, Aunt Farida? What do you want to give me?" Noa's eyes were wide.

"Your mother's diary," Farida said quietly.

They regarded each other in silence. Noa shook off her aunt's hands and wiped her eyes. When she spoke, her voice was a combination of surprise and fury. "A diary . . . what kind of diary? What are you talking about? Since when was there a diary? Why didn't you tell me about this sooner? How dare you hide this from me?" Noa couldn't believe the person who'd been her protector all her life had cheated her like this. She rose from her chair with such violence that it fell over and clattered against the floor, and she stormed out of the kitchen.

Farida stood, too, as though someone had stabbed her posterior with a pin. She rose so quickly she surprised herself. She stumbled into the small living room after Noa. "My girl, don't be angry with me. You have to understand. Just wait a minute." She reached for her niece's hand, but Noa recoiled, and Farida stepped back.

"You tell me, Noa'le," Farida said. "How could I have given a twenty-year-old girl, a girl who didn't know anything about life, her dead mother's diary? You weren't mature enough; you weren't ready. Even without the diary it wasn't easy for you. To read personal things—confusing things—about one's mother would be hard enough—but for a daughter whose mother had just died?" She held her hand in front of her, open, pleading. So we waited, your father and I, we waited for you to grow up. We waited until we thought you were ready to understand it. I wanted to give you the diary when *you* came to *me*, just like you did today. When you started looking for answers about who your mother really was— when you started looking for your roots. I wanted it to come from you, not from me or your father or anyone else. Do you understand what I'm saying?"

"So the two of you were in this together? Who else knew?"

"A blessing on your head." Farida spoke calmly. "Your father and I were the only ones who knew about your mother's diary, and we decided not to tell anyone else about it because we didn't want you and Guy to feel like everyone was hiding something from you. Listen," Farida said. She again tried to place her hands on Noa's shoulders, but Noa wouldn't let her. "When your mother started writing, she had no idea what would happen to her. Listen to me very carefully: in the beginning, your mother wrote only for herself—that's what she told me. It's not easy being sick, and writing allowed her to express her feelings. Later, though, she wrote for you."

Farida raised her hands to the heavens. "Do you understand? Your mother, God have mercy on her soul, kept this diary for you and for Guy. She made both your father and me swear we wouldn't give it to you until you were older. Those were her exact words. She said to me, 'Farida, I'm counting on you and Dan to give this diary to Noa only when you're sure she can appreciate what's inside.'"

Noa's expression softened, and Farida continued.

"This diary, it has everything she ever wanted to tell you. She wanted you to know, that's what she told me, may I fall down dead if I'm not telling the truth. Some of the stories you've already heard, from me or from her, but your mother wanted you to learn about her whole life. She wanted you to know the story of our family. She thought that when you and Guy had families of your own, you'd want to know, but that until then you were too young to care. Someday, she thought, you might want to know more, and who knew if she'd be around to tell you herself? Those were her exact words. So please understand"—she reached for Noa's hand, and this time Noa didn't flinch—"it was for your own good. It was never my intention to take this diary to the grave. I was just waiting for the right moment, and now that moment has come. Do you see now?" Her voice had risen as she talked, and she was nearly shouting. It hadn't been easy to keep the secret. She had been tempted to give it to Noa many times, and she and Dan had almost done so on more than one occasion, but, in the end, neither of them believed Noa was ready. But now the time had come.

"I don't believe this," Noa cried out. Again, tears flooded her eyes, choked her throat. "I want to see this diary! Where is it? Where did you put it? And," she added, "why do you have it in the first place?"

Chapter Five: Farida

After Noa left, Farida stood at the kitchen window for a long time, looking out into the black, moonless night. Hoping to relieve her anxiety, she lit a cigarette, one of the cheap Silons that were so hard to find, and leaned heavily against the window. She drew smoke into her lungs and tried to calm her mind. Silverware and cutlery lay strewn on the table, a thin film of flour covered the floor, and the sink overflowed with dishes. She normally cleaned everything after finishing her cooking and baking, but tonight she let it all sit.

She considered how the diary would affect Noa. Doubts encroached on her mind. Dan had entrusted her with the diary years ago; she had asked for it. They traded it back and forth, depending on who needed it more. Each time the precious notebook passed from one of them to the other, they reaffirmed their commitment: when the time was right, they would give the diary to Noa. Although Farida felt her intuition was nearly infallible, doubt seized her. She wasn't convinced Noa could read the diary and truly understand what it meant, its significance. She wanted Noa to learn about her mother's life, her roots, but she wasn't sure her niece was mature enough to appreciate the beauty of her mother's culture. Her hope was that the diary would make Noa feel closer to Violet, and, in the process, ease Noa's pain. But Farida worried she shouldn't have surrendered the diary when Noa was so tormented, so caught up in her own thoughts. Perhaps she should have waited. Of course, maybe the diary was exactly what Noa needed to find peace. Maybe knowing more about her mother, even if she didn't understand all of it, would provide answers to some of Noa's questions. These and other thoughts trampled through Farida's head, and she was unable to reach any conclusion.

Her sister's image materialized before her eyes. It had been six years without Violet, and her absence was still so acute. She and Violet, the youngest daughters of the family. Though Violet was but slightly older, she played the role of big sister. They were inseparable. Violet was the family rebel, and Farida forever shadowed her. As children, they shared a room; they were together in the kibbutz, first in a tent and later in a small apartment. As young girls in Baghdad, when Farida lay awake through the long, cold, dusty winter nights, Violet told her forlorn stories about separated lovers, lame and lonely dogs searching for affection, and desert bandits who roamed by night and attacked by day.

Winter mornings in the desert brought bitter cold, both inside the house and out. Violet, an early riser, would climb from bed, dress, brush her teeth, and go downstairs to make sandwiches for her and Farida to take to school. Then she would pick out clothes for her younger sister, bring them to their room, climb into Farida's bed, and keep her warm until she was completely dressed. She combed her sister's hair, and the two of them would go off to school. Whenever they were late—which was often, since Farida always stretched the time in her warm bed to the last minute—Violet begged the guard to let her little sister in while she remained outside, bearing the punishment herself.

When Farida thought about Violet, she felt her standing right there, felt the soft, kind touch of her sister's hands. She closed her eyes and succumbed to the feeling of her sister's lips kissing her head, protecting her even now. Violet shouldn't have left this world the way she did, Farida thought bitterly. Violet was the symbol of a joyful family life, with a dancing smile forever on her lips.

What a miserable, heartbreaking end her beloved sister had met, thought Farida. And now, what was left in this world? Violet was gone, Eddie was gone, and her own Moshe had passed two years ago. How much pain could one person endure and still get out of bed every morning? Farida was overcome by a searing loneliness: her own generation was dying out, the younger generation grew increasingly distant, everyone was busy with their own problems, and what would become of her? She moved to the armchair on the front porch and sank into it. She lit another cigarette, sighed deeply, and leaned back. Tomorrow was a new day. Tomorrow the grandchildren would come. A tiny smile buoyed her lips when she thought of the two children and the noisy laughter that would fill the emptiness in her apartment, the emptiness in her heart.

Chapter Six: Violet

Wednesday, October 17, 1986

The ten days that followed my father's decree—my "Ten Days of Repentance"—were not too bad. I spent my time daydreaming and getting excited: my nephew Eddie's Bar Mitzvah was fast approaching. Eddie was thirteen—it was hard to believe he was growing up. I wondered whether he would still play with me and Farida.

Eddie was an object of adoration for us. His kindness, intelligence, wildness, everything about him thrilled us. I was a year younger than him and one-and-a-half years older than Farida, and the two of them were my whole world.

Eddie, Eddie, Eddie. Whenever I think of him, my heart aches with the same intensity as when we discovered we had lost him.

Eddie always knew exactly what to say. He was the only one of us kids allowed to attend movies by himself (we were girls, and the other boys in the family were too young), and when he returned from a film, he would describe every scene, every detail. Eddie made his own movies, too, just for us. He'd cut pictures from newspapers and project them onto a homemade screen; he was so good at cycling the images it felt like watching a real movie. He sewed a cloth curtain to cover the screen, and he'd wait until we all sat down, breathlessly waiting for the movie to begin, before removing it. He even made sure there were snacks at intermission: something sweet made by one of our mothers.

Eddie had a marvelous sense of humor, an uncanny memory for jokes, and a gift for impersonation. He mimicked teachers at school, *Ima's* friends . . . nobody could resist his magic. Whenever I cried, Eddie made me laugh, and when I was bored, he entertained me. He was my best friend, and he, Farida, and I made a joyful trio.

When the evening before the big event finally arrived, we stood on the roof and kept a vigilant watch for my father's sister, Aunt Madeline, and his mother, may she rest in peace. Grandmother—I must write about her—was unique. Many years ago, when her kids were still young, my grandfather was sent to fight the Turks in World War One. Although he returned alive, he wasn't the same man. He contracted tuberculosis and could no longer take care of his family. He died when my father was just a boy. My grandmother, a young woman with three small children, did her best to support her little family.

During the war, Grandmother raised chickens in her backyard. She used some of their eggs to feed her children, and the rest she sold. On rare occasions, they ate the birds. When she realized she couldn't support the family with chickens alone, Grandmother went out and bought inexpensive jewelry, material, and lacework.

At night she embroidered garments, and during the day she went from house to house and peddled her wares.

Grandmother traveled through the villages on foot, her merchandise packed on the back of a donkey; she frequently encountered vicious highway robbers. Whenever she heard about a celebration in one family or another, she would find out what the mother wanted, and she would make that wish come true. For one woman, she sewed a dreamlike wedding gown based on a drawing in a British magazine; for another she made a ball gown out of lace and muslin. She fashioned clothes for men and children as well. I must point out that in those days, women like my grandmother were considered peculiar; wandering through villages and selling one's wares was not considered suitable work for women. Those who made a living this way were treated as social outcasts, but my grandmother wasn't concerned with honor and status; she worried about how to feed her children. She didn't want to be a burden on her family, which was poor to begin with.

During my grandmother's era, most widows ended up penniless. Even those left with property were soon destitute, since they had no income aside from what their husbands left them. But Grandmother wasn't like other women. Circumstances, you could say, made her a feminist. In addition to the financial hardships, tragedy seemed to pursue her. Grandmother lost her eldest son when an oil lamp set his robe on fire. My father, her second son, started accompanying her at a young age, traveling with her, helping carry her goods. When he grew up, he opened a small store and sold their wares.

My mother, a strong, proud woman, never forgave my father's mother for her low social status. She herself came from a rabbinic family on one side and a wealthy family on the other. Although my father was learned, there was a sense that my mother felt he wasn't really worthy of her. And as for this old, simple woman who would be her mother-in-law . . . well, that was too much for her to bear. My mother didn't see any good in her. She tended to look more at the envelope than at the letter inside. For my part, I loved my kind grandmother, and now, with the wisdom of years, I can say that she was worthy of admiration.

My father spoke seven languages *al burian*, fluently. While working with my grandmother, he decided to study business administration. He was quite talented, and the government hired him for a high-ranking position. In 1930s and 40s Iraq, civil service was an honorable profession, second only to doctors and bank officers. My father, a very quick thinker, stayed in his coveted position for many years, until the birth of the State of Israel. Many Jews lost their jobs after the formation of the Jewish state, not just him. In any case, my father won my mother's heart, partly because of his intelligence, and partly because he knew how to play the *ud*—the fat-bellied guitar so popular in those days.

My mother selected her own husband, which was not the custom back then. Traditionally, the girl's parents chose a groom for their daughter. My mother, the eldest daughter of the most learned and revered man in the village, liked to say she had grown up "like a son." Her father—my grandfather—admired his daughter's cleverness and worshiped the ground on which she walked. He asked her advice and considered her opinions when making decisions. In the end, my mother never forgave herself for marrying someone from such a lowly family. When they lived in Baghdad, she still showed him some respect, but that all changed when they moved to Israel and she—who was used to a life of luxury—was forced to live in a tent and, later, a crowded apartment.

From everything you've just read, you can probably understand why I saw Grandmother so infrequently. I admired and loved her. She had life experience. She told spellbinding stories about her travels, about the different women she met and thieves she eluded. She was warm and open-hearted, and, best of all, she made me the most magnificent dresses, with muslin trim, in the latest London fashions. I longed for her visits. My father's sister Madeline, on the other hand, I didn't like at all. Aunt Madeline was conceited, and she considered children bothersome. I think I disliked her primarily because of one infamous story, the stain on our family's name: she had insulted my mother by rejecting her dowry.

Young people today, at the end of the second millennium, have a hard time grasping the magnitude of the insult, but in Iraqi families, the custom was for the bride to give her in-laws a dowry her parents had saved from the day she was born. My mother's parents worked especially hard, since she was their first daughter after several miscarriages. Iraq in the early 1900s didn't have the same health standards we have today, and a lot of babies died either at birth or soon thereafter. As the eldest daughter, my mother was her father's favorite; in fact, the entire family doted upon her. My grandfather invested a great deal in her dowry. He made sure it was lavish, with elegant furniture, napkins woven with lace and gold, summer and winter curtains, anything a young couple might desire for their new home. The dowry was loaded onto a large wagon and conducted to the groom's home for approval.

The glorious dowry of the daughter of Reuven was sent off with a flurry of trills from all the neighbors, Arab and Jewish alike. It traveled from the poor side of the Jewish neighborhood to the rich side. Aunt Madeline, who was jealous and bitter and had never made a life for herself, who never had a family of her own, who always followed my father, decided the dowry was insufficient. Without telling my grandfather, she sent it back to my grandparents' house. The neighbors saw the wagon return and understood what had happened. They beat their chests and shrieked, "*Ya buya, Ya buya,* something terrible has happened! They've broken up!" The rejection of a dowry was considered a grave insult, and my mother never forgave my aunt for this abasement. Following an abject apology from my father's parents, during which they did their best to reduce the ignominy through ingratiation, preparation for the marriage finally resumed. Right before the wedding my father got a job in Baghdad—the big city. My mother was relieved; she wouldn't have to see the evil Madeline's face on a daily basis, nor those of her brazen parents-in-law.

I'm happy I committed all of this to paper. One day it will assume a different meaning for the young generation that knew nothing about life in Iraq. I feel compelled to write this for the sake of future generations. If my generation doesn't recount the story of The Exodus from Iraq, nothing will be known about our culture, nothing will remain. But now I'm tired. I'll write more another time.

Chapter Seven:
Farida and Ruthie

The following day, Sigal and her two children, Ruthie and Shai, paid a visit to Farida. Farida hugged and kissed them all. After everyone ate, Sigal and Shai lay down to rest in Farida's bedroom.

"Come here, Ruthie," said Farida. "Let's take some *machbuz* and chai *(tea in Arabic)* into the living room and have a private tea party, just the two of us. What do you say?"

"Oh, what fun, Grandmother! You have the best ideas. I love visiting you," said Ruthie. "I miss you so much when we're apart, and I count the days until we see each other again. This time it was five whole days! From Saturday until today. Every day I ask *Ima* when we can visit you, and every day *Ima* says, 'Tomorrow.'"

"I also count the days between visits, my sweet soul, may God bless you, a blessing on your head," said Farida. She held her granddaughter close and breathed in her sweet smell. "There's nothing we can do, my Ruthie. This is how it is. You're a big girl now, and you understand your mother works hard so you and your brother Shai can have a good life. Since your parents split up, things are tougher for Sigal. If I lived closer, I could do more, but now it's up to you to help as much as you can."

"Yes," Ruthie said, taking a deep breath. "I do help her, but I don't understand why I'm always counting days. I count the days until I see my father, then I count the days before I see you. Ugh, I cannot stand counting days." She looked at Farida, searching for answers she rarely got from adults.

"My sweet one, I know it's not easy for you." Farida felt pangs of anguish for her small granddaughter. "Would you like me to read you a book, my love? I bought you a new Caspian. You like Paul Kor's books, right? Come, look at this. *Caspian's Great Journey.*"

"Caspian?" said Ruthie, rolling her eyes. "Caspian is a baby book. Read it to Shai." She gave a truculent shake of the head, but then turned a pleading look on Farida. "But can you tell me more about what it was like when you were a little girl? You know how much I love your stories, Grandmother."

"Oh, fine." Farida's smile lit up her face, and she nuzzled her nose into Ruthie's cheek. "How can I refuse those gorgeous eyes and that adorable nose? Okay. So which story do you want to hear today?"

"Umm . . ." Ruthie thought for a moment, then said, "Maybe you can tell me about Noa's mother, Aunt Violet. I love to hear about the silly things you used to do together. Okay?"

"Alright. You're the boss, Munchkin." Farida saluted her granddaughter. "I will tell you anything you want to know. In fact," she said, placing her hands on her granddaughter's shoulders. "Today I'm going to tell you about a very special person's Bar Mitzvah."

"Whose Bar Mitzvah, Grandmother? Whose?"

"It's someone you don't know." Farida led Ruthie to the bulky living room sofa. "Did you know that Grandmother Habiba had a son named Edward?"

"You mean Grandmother Candy, with the funny nose?" asked Ruthie.

"Yes." Farida smiled. "Grandmother Candy, who always has candies in her purse. And you're right, she does have a funny nose. But," she said, "don't ever tell her that—she'd be very offended." She wagged her finger at Ruthie, half joking and half threatening.

"Okay, I promise," said Ruthie. "Now can you please get on with it?"

"Alright," Farida began. "I'll start by telling you who Edward was, then I'll tell you about his Bar Mitzvah. Deal?"

"Deal," Ruthie said, her eyes shining.

"Edward was Grandmother Habiba's son," Farida said. "He was older than me. Now I know you're going to laugh"—she took Ruthie's hands in hers—"he was two or three years older than me, but I was his aunt, and he was—what's the word? my nephew. This must be very confusing. Listen," she said. "I'll tell you how it happened." Ruthie's hands nestled in her grandmother's. "In Iraq, people got married very young, and they had children very young, and sometimes"—she shot Ruthie a serious look—"not often, but sometimes, your best friend can also be your uncle. A mother and her daughter can even be pregnant at the same time . . ." Farida laughed, and Ruthie looked at her, completely befuddled. "That's how it was with us. We weren't even the same age—he

51

was older than me, but I was his aunt. Does any of this make sense to you?"

"A little bit," giggled Ruthie. "Grandmother, are you saying you wanted to marry your nephew?"

"I wanted to, yes, but it didn't turn out that way." Farida sighed. "I know it must seem strange in this day and age, but that's how it was back then. Sometimes people married their relatives. There were families that preferred it that way; they knew the groom, they knew his mother and father. It was just easier—do you see?"

"A little bit—it doesn't matter, just go on, Grandmother. Tell me about Edward." Ruthie didn't care about lineage; she was just happy to be so close to her grandmother.

"Everyone called him Eddie," said Farida, "because Edward seemed like a long name for a little boy. He was my very best friend. He was fun . . . or, as you say, 'cool.'"

"But Grandmother," said Ruthie, cocking her head. "You once told
me that Violet was your best friend."

"Yes, you're right. Violet was my best *girl*friend." She stroked her granddaughter's hair. "But Eddie was my best boyfriend."

"Okay. Now I get it. Now . . . oh, whatever, just go on." Ruthie nuzzled closer.

"Eddie was smart, and as handsome as a Swede," said Farida, her face lighting up like that of a ten-year old falling in love for the first time. "He looked like my grandfather: blonde with the greenest eyes, the exact color of your shirt." Farida sighed deeply, then looked down at her granddaughter. She squared her shoulders and went on.

"The three of us were, well, our own little circle. We did all kinds of silly things. Sometimes we did things that were downright dangerous. Thinking back, I can't understand how nothing bad ever happened to us. I hope you will behave better than we did," she added with a grin.

"Grandmother, I already behave—ask Mom. I help her take care of Shai, and I never get into trouble," said Ruthie, her proud chin jutting forth.

"Yes. I know you are a good girl. Now where were we?"

"The silly things you did."

"We did all kinds of stupid things, but that's a whole other story. Now I want to tell you about Eddie's Bar Mitzvah, which I will never forget as long as I live." Farida brow wrinkled.

"Why not?" asked Ruthie.

"Because it was his Bar Mitzvah, and I was only ten years old, maybe eleven, but I loved him in a way I had never loved anyone before." Farida couldn't believe she was confiding in her granddaughter, who may or may not have understood what she was saying.

"Not even Grandpa?" Ruthie asked, shocked.

"If you promise not to tell anyone what I'm about to tell you, I'll answer your question."

"I promise. I swear to God: I will never tell a soul."

"Okay then," Farida smiled. "I think I can trust you." She took a deep breath and looked down, like a girl caught being naughty. "I loved him even more than I loved your grandfather, may his memory be blessed, and you know how much I loved *him*. Eddie was my first love. When you grow up, you'll understand." She winked at Ruthie. "There's nothing like first love. That stays in your heart forever."

"Ugh, adults always say that," Ruthie complained. "'When you grow up, you'll understand,'" she said, mimicking her grandmother's voice.

"Do you want to be angry, or do you want me to go on?"

"Oh, fine, go on, Grandmother." Ruthie rolled her eyes and exhaled loudly.

"At home, I remember, we spent weeks preparing for the party, which would take place in the winter, right before Chanukah."

"What?" Ruthie asked, stunned. "You had Chanukah in Iraq, too?"

"Of course!" Farida laughed loudly, then quieted as she remembered Sigal and Shai napping in the next room. "People celebrate holidays all over the world, even in Iraq. Chanukah has been around for a long time," she said, stroking Ruthie's face.

"The party was going to be in our house. We had to prepare weeks in advance. We had winter curtains and summer curtains—can you believe it? The summer curtains were white with the most gorgeous embroidery. We took them down and put up the winter curtains, which were also beautiful. They were velvet, like the dress I bought you before your birthday—remember?"

"Which dress, Grandmother? The red one?"

"Yes," said Farida, "the red dress I bought you. It's made from the exact same material as the curtains. You know something? Now that I think about it, every year, before Chanukah, we'd put away our regular menorah, which was the light source for everyday, and replace it with a special one. We did it every year, including the year of the Bar Mitzvah, *allah yirchamu.*" She pointed toward the heavens. "And Eddie's Bar Mitzvah fell right on Chanukah."

Ruthie's eyes shimmered, and her mouth hung open, slack in anticipation. Farida continued: "This menorah, the one we put out for Chanukah and Eddie's Bar Mitzvah, was made of real silver." With her hands, she formed the shape of a candelabrum. "It had nine branches. Ach, what a gorgeous menorah." Longing infused her voice. "I'm telling you, never in my life have I seen a lamp that beautiful. It was truly one-of-a-kind. And the servants had to polish it every year—it took them hours."

"Why?" asked Ruthie.

"Because silver tarnishes over time. If you really want it to shine, you have to scour it with a special solution. When they finished, you could see your face in the menorah—that's how much it sparkled." Farida laughed.

"Wow," said Ruthie. "But where is it now?"

"Ach," Farida muttered. "Who knows? Maybe they sold it in Iraq; maybe someone took it. It didn't come with us; it stayed there. They wouldn't let us bring anything, those Iraqi bastards—they should all go to hell. They barely let us take the clothes on our backs."

"Too bad," Ruthie said, "because the menorah you have now isn't nice at all—"

"Well, that's another matter entirely," Farida snapped. "Do you want me to go on?"

"Of course, Grandmother. Tell me what else you had there."

"I remember . . ." Farida thought back over the span of many years. "I remember that, for Eddie's Bar Mitzvah, we took out the good rugs we had rolled up and stored for the summer. Every year we took the rugs out during summer and packed them up for winter. Do you know why they brought out the rugs?"

"Why?" asked Ruthie, her little eyes wide.

"Because it was very hot in Iraq. Do you remember when we went to Eilat? How hot it was?" She didn't wait for an answer. "In Iraq, it was even hotter. And there were sandstorms that blotted out everything. And my mother didn't want the rugs ruined. But before the Bar Mitzvah, and before Chanukah, she took them out of storage and unfurled them. Ach," she inhaled deeply, "I will never forget those cleaning smells as long as I live. To this day, they're still somewhere inside my nose."

"Where, Grandmother? Show me!" laughed Ruthie, reaching out to press her grandmother's nose.

"Right here!" Farida gently honked her granddaughter's nose. "You know, cleaning the house, that was really something. And the wonderful smells drifting out of the kitchen . . . wow." Again she inhaled, breathing in sweet memories.

"Go on!" Ruthie tugged on her grandmother's shirt. Farida shivered, and her demeanor turned serious.

"There must have been ten servants working in our house, maybe more, just to prepare the feast we needed. And to ready the house for the party." Farida coughed, and the flesh of her large shoulders jiggled. "Most times, we had several servants: one to clean, one to cook, and one to look after me and Violet, and my brothers' children, too . . . She used to play with us, poor thing. Imagine, a girl just a little bit older than you, taking care of so many children, and every one of them driving her crazy. Sometimes she even had to watch Anwar's children, my sister Habiba's children, and my sister Farcha's children. Everyone had little kids, about your age, even younger, and when the grown-ups went out, she looked after us all." Farida put her arms around Ruthie's neck and hugged. After planting several loud, wet kisses on the girl's forehead, she continued. "We even had one servant, a man, who worked for my mother: he shopped, drove the carriage, ran errands . . ."

Ruthie sat, mesmerized. She tried to imagine such a display of wealth and grandeur; in her little mind, the scene was lifted straight out of Cinderella's ball. She looked into her grandmother's eyes, sighed, and said, "If only I lived in Iraq."

These words cut at Farida's heart. "God forbid!" she shouted, warding off the evil eye. "There's more to life than money, Ruthie," she said. "When you grow up, you'll understand. Sure, money's nice, but we didn't want to stay in Baghdad, Ruthie. We wanted to come to the Holy Land. What don't we have here? Gold? Believe me, things are good here. The people in Baghdad are miserable. There's a tyrant over there by the name of Saddam; he kills people right and left, for no reason at all. If he thinks a person said bad things about him, he'll kill him. Do you see, Ruthie? Democracy is more important. It's hard for you to understand, so let me explain it. Democracy is being able to walk through the streets and say whatever you want, without being afraid. Now do you understand? Money isn't everything. This is where we belong. Here, nobody calls you *stinking Jew* when they pass you on the street. Do you understand what this means?"

Ruthie sat, mute, gazing at Farida's impassioned face, listening.

"Ruthie, nothing's like our country, because it's our country. Remember what I'm telling you," she concluded in a decisive voice, "even when you're a big girl."

After a long silence, Farida resumed. "Now, let me tell you about the ball. But just remember: I have never missed Iraq, not once. Deal?"

Although Ruthie didn't really understand what her grandmother meant, she said, "Deal."

"Good. Now I can go on. So, for this party . . ." Once again, Farida's face was calm, with no trace of her recent outburst. "We needed even more help. Everyone sent their servants to our house for several days. You're going to laugh when I tell you which was the hardest job of all."

"Which?" Ruthie was relieved to hear her grandmother's voice return to normal.

"Cleaning the gigantic fish. *Shevit* they were called. Turbot."

"What kind of fish are those?" asked Ruthie. "I've heard of carp. Once, at Grandmother Rosa's house, I saw some carp in the bathtub. We ate them on Rosh Hashanah."

"They're not exactly the same," laughed Farida. She stroked her granddaughter's hair. "*Shevit* are giant fish that live in the rivers of Baghdad. They don't have them here. Should I go on?" She arched her eyebrows.

"Yes, Grandmother," Ruthie said. "Tell me more."

"First, we had to clean the fish; then we had to fry them. And you know why we needed so many?" She didn't wait for an answer. "Because eating fish is a *mitzvah*—a good deed. And do you know why it's a *mitzvah*?"

"No." Ruthie's stared at her grandmother.

"Because fish are a good sign. They bring good luck—the more fish, the better. Also, whenever there was a Bar Mitzvah or a wedding, all the Jews were invited. The poor people would get a hot meal, which is also a *mitzvah*. There were a lot of people to feed."

"But Grandmother, wait a minute." Creases furrowed Ruthie's brow. "Why didn't your mother take care of you?"

"Ah, that's a good question," Farida said. "We were very rich and well-respected in our community. You're right, even though our mother was in charge of the household, it was a servant who bathed and fed us. That's how things were over there. My mother supervised everyone: the kids, the servants, my father." She gave a bitter smile. "My father was in charge of discipline. He was like your school principal. Can you imagine that?"

"My father and mother aren't like that, are they?" Ruthie asked.

"No," Farida smiled. "Definitely not. But things were different in those days. My father was one of the most important men in the community; people trembled in his presence. As for my mother, well, my mother was always busy, going to tea parties, visiting her neighbors, someone was born, someone died . . . she was hardly ever at home. She also liked to entertain. Anyone lucky enough to receive an invitation to our house was considered important, because he had been hosted by *Um Anwar*. That's what they used to call my mother. It means 'Mother of Anwar'—Anwar was her first-born son. My sister Farcha, who was already married with children of her own, also rarely took care of her kids. She was busy going with my grandmother, Samira, to many different parties."

"And your mother never missed you?" Ruthie had a puzzled look on her face. "When my mother comes home from work, she always tells me how much she missed me. But my mother has to work, she says. So why did your mother leave you all the time?"

"A blessing on your head—what a smart girl you are," said Farida in amazement. "You're right; your mother does miss you all the time. But that's how it was when I was a girl. In Iraq it was all about social status. The more servants you had, the more respected you were. My mother almost never hugged and kissed us; she was too preoccupied with her own affairs. But you know what? Even though she wasn't with us, it felt like her eyes followed us everywhere. She always knew exactly what we were up to, and if, God forbid, someone was sick, she always took care of that child herself. But raising children? I just don't think it interested her. Okay, enough of that, Ruthie. That's the way things were. Do you still want to live in Iraq?"

"No," Ruthie said. "Absolutely not. But go on about the party. What was it like?"

"Wait a minute—what's the rush? Before I talk about the party itself, I want to tell you some other important things. You know that the winters in Iraq are so cold that water freezes in the faucets?"

"No, you never told me that before."

"The winters were brutal. Iraq is a desert, but it was so cold come wintertime that water froze in the pipes, and everything came to a halt."

"Why?" Ruthie asked. "Didn't you like to chew on ice when you were a kid?"

"Of course I did. I still like it to this day. But you're a smart girl—tell me, how can you get water from a faucet if it's frozen inside the pipes? You can't, right? And if you can't get it from the tap, you have to get it from outside, which is very hard work. So the week before the party we prayed the water wouldn't freeze, because if it did, we wouldn't be able to cook anything. And really, we were very lucky it didn't freeze. And another thing. The night before the party, we were so excited. We were waiting for our grandmother, my father's mother, and for Aunt Madeline, my father's sister. They were coming on the train from Basra, another city a long way from Baghdad. The ride took hours, and then, to get to our house, they had to travel by carriage."

"Carriages with horses, like the ones we went on in Netanya?" said Ruthie.

"Yes, a lot like the ones in Netanya. That's how people traveled from one place to another; they used them all the time, like we use cars today. Every evening, at exactly the same time, the train arrived at the station, which was near our house. We heard the whistle when it pulled into the station, And then the sound of whips as the horses pulled the carriages."

"Wow!"

"You know, our house was always open to guests. All the carriage drivers knew that if a Jew came from far away and didn't have a place to sleep, he'd be able to stay with us. My mother, while a terrible snob toward people in our community, welcomed strangers graciously. You know what a snob is, right?"

"I think so, Grandmother," Ruthie said. "A snob is someone with her nose in the air—that's what my friend Noga says. Like this." Ruthie lifted her nose and laughed.

"That looks like a pig's nose!" Farida laughed, too. She gave her granddaughter a wet kiss on the cheek. "Should we go on?"

"Of course, Grandmother. This is a great story."

"Okay. So," Farida said, "there were nights when we heard the horsewhips coming closer. That's when we knew someone was coming to stay with us. But that evening, we knew who was coming: not just any old guests, but Grandmother and Aunt Madeline. So we sat there and waited, and every time we thought we heard the horsewhips, we jumped from our seats. I remember I missed my grandmother fiercely. I hadn't seen her for half a year—a long, long time."

Farida looked at the sweet, small face staring at her, enraptured. For a moment, she felt like she herself was a child talking to her sister Violet. She vividly remembered that night, the night before Eddie's Bar Mitzvah. She was almost eleven, and she missed her grandmother terribly. She hadn't thought about her grandmother in years. To Farida's dismay, the feeling disappeared as quickly as it had come. She went back to her story.

"You have to understand, Ruthie," she explained solemnly. "Our lives in Iraq were nothing like our lives today. Here, we get into a car and drive for five minutes. There, if you didn't live very close to people, you hardly ever saw them. You'd see them at weddings, maybe, and

63

brits, sometimes on holidays. Once a year, more or less. That's how it was. My father's family lived in a different city: Basra. Like I said, it was far away. That's why I was so excited about my grandmother's visit."

"We are lucky to live in Israel. Very lucky," said Ruthie with a solemn look. Farida broke out into a broad smile. Ruthie, waiting in suspense, asked, "Then what happened? Did they get there?"

"Of course they did," Farida said. "And when they got there, we all went downstairs to greet them. The kids got out of bed and ran, and the reunion with Grandmother, it was so emotional, you wouldn't believe how much hugging and kissing . . . My grandmother gave me a bear hug, just like I give you when you come over. Like this." She pressed Ruthie to her chest in a hug so tight it almost suffocated the child.

"I get the idea!" Ruthie said, laughing. "Stop, you're practically choking me."

Farida laughed, too. She loved telling Ruthie these stories about her family. She was so happy; it was hard to tell which of them enjoyed the stories more. When their laughter died down, Farida continued.

"Eddie got so many Bar Mitzvah presents. Grandmother made him three suits: one for being called to the Torah, one for the special ceremony of tying the *Tefillin* to the head and to the arm, and one for the party, which I'll tell you about in a minute. My grandmother didn't forget anyone; she brought all kinds of goodies. You know what we got?"

"What? Did she bring you candy? I love candy," Ruthie said dreamily. "Did you get a lot of candy?"

"No," said Farida. "We didn't get any candy at all. When I was a kid, 'candy' meant dried fruit: figs, dates, raisins, and tamarind, which is kind of sour. Even those were a rare treat. Oh, I remember now. My grandmother also brought *mlabas*. Do you know what those are?" Farida couldn't wait for an answer; once again, she was a small child, savoring many tastes. "It's a sweet, sticky kind of delicacy, filled with almonds. Sometimes I buy Iraqi treats at Ezra's shop downtown. But they're not the same."

"Oh," she went on, "how we waited for something sweet . . . On very rare occasions, we got foreign chocolate, if we had a guest from England or something. But for my grandmother, *Allah yirchama (may God bless her memory)*, nothing was too good for us. That day, we even got chocolate, which to this day I can still taste."

"Yum," Ruthie said, licking her lips. "Me, too."

"The next morning, after everyone got ready, we gathered in the parlor. Eddie had put together a whole performance for all the important guests. What can I tell you?" Farida tapped her thigh, and her face was radiant. "Eddie was a master. The plays he would put on! Sometimes he even made movies with us. He organized the whole thing himself. He'd write the story—the screenplay, it's called; he'd cut pictures out of newspapers and glue them to paper, one after the other. You know, we didn't have television back then, and Eddie was the only one allowed to go to the movies."

"Why?" Ruthie asked.

"That's how it was when I was a kid," she said, waving her hand. "Eddie was a boy, but Violet and I were girls, so we weren't allowed to attend movies. The other boys in the family were too young. But hold on a minute—where was I?"

"At the play, Grandmother," Ruthie said. "Did you forget already?"

"Oh, yes, that's right." Farida returned to her memories. "So Eddie put on a special play in honor of his Bar Mitzvah. He played the lead role, and he was in love with the lead actress—you know what the lead is, right?"

"Not exactly," Ruthie said.

"Well, if you don't know, you have to ask, okay?" Farida pursed her lips.

"Fine. So what's the lead?"

"The lead is the most important actor in the play. He's kind of in charge of all the other actors, understand? And who do you think the lead actress was?"

"The lead actress is like the lead actor, right, only she's a girl?" asked Ruthie.

"That's right. God bless you—how smart you are."

"So who was the lead actress?" Ruthie asked.

"Me." Farida pointed to herself with pride. "Eddie played the role of someone in love with me. And me? I was thrilled, I was just thrilled. I was in heaven. You know why?" Again, she didn't wait for an answer. She leaned in close to her granddaughter. "Because I was in love with him," she whispered. "But like I told you, that's our little secret, right?"

"Yes, Grandmother. I already promised you." Ruthie pretended to zip her lips. "But if you were in love with him why didn't you marry him?"

"Wait a minute, my little one," Farida sighed. "That's a long, long story, which I'll tell you another time."

"First tell me about the play."

Farida happily continued: "So this is what happened. The two of us, Eddie and I, we were the stars of the show, like I said. There were other actors, too. For example, the parents of the happy couple were played by two of my girlfriends. They borrowed clothes from their parents. We all worked so hard; people couldn't wait to see our shows," Farida bragged. "What didn't we have in that play? We had an evil old uncle played by Farcha's oldest son Danny—you've met him. He was younger than us. I think I've named all the actors . . . what a plot, *ya walli*, such a sad story about love, heartbreaking, really. I even sang some songs by Leila Mourad—she was a famous vocalist. And Eddie sang songs by another famous singer: Abd al-Wahhab."

"Oh, Grandmother, that sounds so nice. Do you think we can put on a play for Mommy and Shai when they wake up?"

"That's not a bad idea," Farida smiled, "but not today, okay? I mean, if we're going to do a play, we might as well do it right. With costumes and everything." She winked at her granddaughter and continued: "Well, nobody missed this play. Everyone was looking forward to it: my father and mother, and Anwar, and my sisters, and of course all of their kids, and Aunt Madeline, and Grandmother, even the neighbors. We rehearsed and rehearsed, *ya binati*, until we were absolutely certain we were ready. Then we made invitations for neighbors and friends, for family, and for all the important guests. We wrote, 'You are invited to the most important, earth-shattering show in the world.'" Farida said like a town crier; she waved her hands in invitation. "Everyone was invited. 'Bring handkerchiefs,' we told them, 'there will be much crying.'" Farida chuckled, then succumbed to a fit of laughter that brought tears to her eyes.

The bedroom door opened, and Sigal joined them. "Oh," Farida said apologetically, "I see *Ima* has woken up."

"But you still haven't told me anything about this Bar Mitzvah," said Ruthie.

"That's not so bad, Ruthie, a blessing on your head," Farida said. "Next time we'll pick up right where we left off. Now come with me and we'll make your *Ima* some coffee, okay?" And with that, she plodded off to the kitchen.

Chapter Eight: The Bar Mitzvah

Thursday, October 18, 1986

Back to my nephew Eddie's Bar Mitzvah—the Bar Mitzvah that was one of the highlights of my life. "Grandmother's here!" we all cried from the rooftop. "Grandmother's here!" We ran downstairs to greet her, and I threw my arms around her neck. My beloved grandmother held me to her chest and whispered she loved me, that she'd brought a gorgeous dress made just for me, a dress I could wear to the fancy party that followed the regular celebration. "Oh, Grandmother," I whispered in her ear, "thank you! I missed you so much . . ." My parents also came down to welcome their guests; then we all went inside. The house was ready for the Bar Mitzvah.

When I look back at the party, after all these years, I realize Eddie didn't really want to be the center of attention. Every chance he got, he evaded the commotion, slipping out to ride his new bicycle, a gift from Richie's parents. Richie, Eddie's best friend, was the son of Mr. Hardy, my father's boss. The Hardys lived in England and were only in Iraq temporarily. Iraq was administered via British Mandate back then, and Mr. Hardy was the manager of the Department of Water and Agriculture. The primary function of this department was to protect the Chidekel River from flooding. My father's division was responsible for stockpiling sandbags, wood, bags of cement—materials that would allow citizens to protect homes and property when the river flooded, which occurred almost yearly. *Aba* was the department's chief accountant, and it was his job that was responsible for our family moving to the big city.

Eddie and Richie were best friends. They'd meet after school and hang out in the Hardy mansion's courtyard. They went to movies and plays, and they fantasized about girls. Eddie dreamed of Farida; even then, he was in love with her. Farida was a real beauty: raven hair; alabaster skin; big, dark, curious eyes. Her good nature was apparent to everyone. In her heart, Farida was *Ima's* good girl, but because she tried to emulate me, she got into trouble.

For the *tefillin* ceremony—the first time Eddie wore phylacteries—people thronged the house. We all wore our finest clothes. Grandmother made two dresses for Farida and me, one for each party. For the *hanachat tefillin*, we both wore white muslin gowns with long pink sashes. Our evening frocks were made of velvet. Farida's was blue with white trim, and mine was purple, to highlight the paleness of my skin. Eddie wore a suit to both events, but he changed ties; he seemed very confused. My sister Habiba looked resplendent, and she was very emotional. This was her eldest son's Bar Mitzvah, the first of the grandsons. Habiba was a young mother; she was only thirty-one when Eddie celebrated his Bar Mitzvah. Today, women her age are just starting to become mothers.

When Farida looked at Eddie, her eyes sparkled with pride and happiness. He was sneaking glances at her, too. When he first donned his *tefillin*, the women trilled with joy. Eddie didn't make a single mistake. Afterward, the rabbi of our community, Chacham Sasson, spoke of the importance of *tefillin* and Eddie's responsibilities henceforth. Even after all these years, I still remember the details. That day is etched in my memory forever.

Chacham Sasson blessed the entire family and wished Eddie health, wisdom, and a long life. And he blessed himself as well, asking for the privilege of attending Eddie's future wedding. When the rabbi talked of Eddie's wedding, Farida blushed. I remember monitoring her reactions. Her love for Eddie was a secret, and she hadn't exactly told me about her feelings, but she always was—and still is—unable to hide things from me. Years later, Farida told me that on that day, when she was not even eleven years old, she imagined herself and Eddie standing under the wedding canopy, Chacham Sasson officiating. She dreamt of that day; she hoped and prayed for it. My father's grandmother was betrothed at the age of nine, married at twelve, and had her first son at fourteen, so it felt natural to be in love at such a young age, even planning a wedding.

After the *tefillin* ceremony, it was time for the festive meal we'd planned so long for. The tables stood stacked with delicacies: all variety of meat and fish, vegetables, fresh fruit, dried fruit, different kinds of pickles—like *mkhalela*, turnips steeped in saltwater—and *tum ajam*—garlic marinated in salt and curry. Everyone enjoyed the lavish hospitality and gorged themselves. We kids focused on the desserts served after the meal, which included all the sweets we loved so much. We stuffed ourselves with ginger, marzipan, baklava, and *mlabas*. These days, I still go to Petach Tikvah every now and then to buy these treats, usually right before Purim.

After the big meal, we capped the glorious day with a European-style dance party—a Bar Mitzvah gift from my parents (Eddie's grandparents) to Habiba and her husband.

My mother, whose expertise and authority made her the natural choice, was in charge of putting together the impressive invitation list. Needless to say, it included all of the Baghdad bigwigs, many of whom were not Jewish. We waltzed, tangoed, and danced all of the couples dances just becoming popular at Iraqi-Jewish parties. The men wore elegant suits, and the women were garbed in fantastic dresses modeled on Paris and London catalogues and made by the best seamstresses in Iraq. Farida and I, in the dresses made by our grandmother, looked much older than we were, which made us giddy. We waited nervously for men to ask us to dance.

I will never forget the excitement that seized us that day. Farida, I remember, was even more emotional than I was. Around her neck she wore our mother's pearl necklace, and her blue dress brought out her lovely dark eyes. She pinched her cheeks to make them red, outshining the other girls at the party. Eddie wore his Bar Mitzvah suit, with a flower in his lapel. He wasn't accustomed to these kinds of festivities and acted very flustered, although it may have been Farida's beauty that stunned and unnerved him. Her looks certainly had the same effect on the other boys. Eddie couldn't stop watching her. He was good-looking, with an attractive personality, and, because he came from a well-known and respected family, he was considered an excellent match. Many girls vied for his attention, but it didn't matter. Farida was the only one who interested him.

Farida stood next to our mother, waiting for an invitation to dance. I'm sure she secretly hoped Eddie would approach her. I danced with neighborhood boys. I felt radiant; my dress accentuated my body, and my long hair, usually tied back, was loose. I felt womanly, no longer a little girl playing in the mud, running around, getting into trouble, but practically a real woman. And Eddie . . . Well, Eddie asked Farida. He danced the first dance with her, and the second, then the third and the fourth. Eddie danced with her the entire night. Their feelings were so intense they were on the verge of tears. This was the first time Eddie's face was so close to Farida's, the first time they'd touched like this—not as part of a game, not as a way to annoy each other. This was different: a mature touch, a loving touch. I heard *Ima* whisper to *Aba* that they'd have to pay closer attention to the kids, to their eldest grandson and their youngest daughter. Many romantic relationships between family members weren't seen as peculiar back then—forty-five years ago in Iraq there were marriages between cousins, between uncles and nieces. But with

Eddie and Farida, something wasn't right. Marriages between nephews and aunts, those were unusual.

In any case, it was Farida and Eddie's night. I remember it in great detail. Maybe because the two of them were so close to me, or maybe because I envied them. I, who had always formed a vital part of our happy trio, was left out.

Chapter Nine: Noa

Ofir

Noa returned to her small dorm room exhausted; it had been a long day. Her roommate, Ofir, wasn't home, and she was glad. She wasn't in the mood for small talk. The diary was buried deep inside her bag. Noa wasn't planning to look at it just yet, at least not that night. She was too distraught. The existence of the secret diary had turned her world upside-down, and she didn't think she had the emotional fortitude to read it. She lay on her shabby sofa, facing the wall, sinking in memories.

Images floated before her eyes: a hug from her mother at her kindergarten birthday party; her parents arguing like children about something trivial when she was ten or eleven; her parents reconciling, kissing, drawing her into their embrace. She recalled one time when she was almost twelve, almost a Bat-Mitzvah, and her brother Guy was chasing her around, trying to tickle her, and she couldn't get away because she was laughing so hard, and Guy caught her right away. Her mother complained they were being too rambunctious, preventing her from working, but she couldn't help being swept up in their silliness, and in the end both Noa and Guy pounced on Violet and tickled her. She remembered her father telling her about her mother's illness; she didn't really understand. She was fourteen years old. Her mother looked ashen, but tried to act like nothing was wrong, like nothing would ever be wrong. Everything was normal, no cause for worry, her parents told her. Her mother was strong. She'd prevail over any illness.

Noa's mother rose with the children every morning and prepared hot drinks for the whole family. Strong brewed coffee for *Aba*, tea with fresh mint for Guy, and instant coffee with milk for Noa. Noa was already seventeen, and her mother had ceased teaching at the university. She told Noa she'd decided to take a year to research the seclusion of Tel Aviv's ultra-Orthodox community. It sounded strange to Noa, her mother taking an entire year to study something that sounded like a disease. It wasn't until much later that Noa understood the concept of isolation, of seclusion—but even so, she would never have guessed her mother's true condition. Soon after, Noa was drafted, and on the day of her induction, the whole family accompanied her to Tel Hashomer. Noa's mother didn't stop crying, nor did Noa. They embraced for a long time, until Noa had to get on the bus. They had a hard time saying goodbye. And then . . .

Noa didn't hear Ofir enter. She didn't hear him set down his briefcase and call for her. She was so absorbed in her thoughts she didn't realize he was standing next to her, looking at her.

"Noa?"

She jumped up. "Are you crazy, scaring me like that? How long have you been standing there anyway?"

"I'm sorry. I really wasn't trying to scare you." Ofir sounded contrite. "I just walked in. Are you Okay?"

"Why? Do I look like I'm not?" She didn't like others seeing her at her weakest.

"You look fine," Ofir answered, confused. "But you also look a little strange. How could you not have heard me come in?"

"I don't know; I just didn't." Noa tugged down on her shirt, straightening it, and sat back down. "Tell me, how do you know there's something wrong?" She stared up into his face, curious.

"Oh . . . that's easy. Believe it or not, Noa, you're very transparent." Ofir knelt and looked into her eyes. "When you're in a good mood, you can tell from miles away." He gave a thumbs-up then turned his thumb toward the floor, " And when you're in a bad mood, you can also tell from miles away. So what's going on, Noa?" He got off his knees and sat next to her.

Noa debated whether or not to tell Ofir about her evening. She decided she had nothing to hide. She looked down and then spoke. "You won't believe what happened to me today; you just won't believe it."

Ofir sat on an armchair across from her, waiting.

"After my exam, I went to visit my aunt." Noa paused.

"Which aunt? The Iraqi one with the good food, or the native Israeli one who rolls her Rs?" He mimicked their voices as he spoke.

Noa didn't smile. "I was at my Aunt Farida's, the one with the food. And at first it was really nice. You know how aunts are. They pamper you, feed you, ask about you: what's going on, when you're getting married. Then out of nowhere they give you a diary you didn't know existed and send you home with enough food for a week."

"So far it doesn't sound so bad. What are you complaining about? At least we have Iraqi food, and we don't have to cook. So she asked you when you're getting married? For a week's worth of food, that doesn't seem like such a high price to pay." There was a mischievous sparkle in his eyes, and he was smiling. "Wait a second." He cut himself off. "Did you say a diary? Whose? Yours?"

"No, Ofir, not mine. It was my mother's," Noa whispered.

"Wow," Ofir muttered, this time without a trace of humor. "That's really something." He hung his head. "So?" he said. "What did it say?" When she didn't respond, he asked softly, "Did you have a chance to read any of it?"

"No, I couldn't bring myself to read it. I don't think I'm strong enough right now."

"I understand," he said. After a moment, he corrected himself. "Actually, no, I don't understand why you wouldn't want to read it . . . I mean, you don't look particularly weak. I'm tripping over myself here, but I guess what I'm saying is that you are really a very strong human being."

"Thank you, Ofir. You're a good friend." She smiled. "It's just that right now, I feel like my whole life is turning upside-down."

"You don't seem to be standing on your head," he said.

"Enough." Noa was losing patience. "I'm really not in the mood for your humor."

Ofir took hold of Noa's hands, pressed them to his chest, and said, "I understand how hard things are, and to complicate them even further, I will ask you a difficult and enigmatic question: would Mademoiselle Rosen be so kind as to accompany me to a geek party at the *moshav* next Friday?"

"Ofir, you are such a character," Noa said, laughing. "A geek party at an agricultural settlement? I have no idea how you do it,"

"Look, I made you smile," Ofir said, beaming.

"Which *moshav*?"

"Up in the Sharon Valley—what, you think it matters which one? All those farming villages look the same to me."

"What can I say, Ofir? As tempting and exciting as it sounds, accompanying you to a geek party somewhere up north . . . no, I'm afraid not."

"And if I beg you to come with me, then will you agree? The truth is I asked about half the women in the city," he said, "and nobody wanted to come with me, so as you can see, I'm truly desperate . . ." His smile was hard to resist.

"Okay, if you beg, I'll come." Noa laughed.

"Well, I'm begging. Should I get down on my knees?"

"No," Noa said, "but if you make me a cup of coffee, the way I like it, I'll call it even." She couldn't understand how Ofir always managed to lift her spirits.

He didn't mention the diary again, and neither did Noa. She lay awake half the night trying to decide what to do. She put the diary under her pillow, and it felt like her mother was with her, keeping company, watching over her. Noa feared what she might find inside the journal. She was afraid of guilt that might consume her, of discovering a different mother than the one she had known. She wondered if perhaps she should just enjoy her mother's presence and be content with that. There, under the pillow, lay something that contained her mother's entire world.

Ehud

The next morning, Noa woke up with a peculiar feeling. It seemed like the diary under her pillow had lulled her into a deep, dreamless sleep. She stretched her limbs luxuriously and looked out the window at the street below. Warm sun rays caressed her face.

Noa smiled. She leaned on the windowsill, thinking that the world was beautiful. She had finished her exams and could finally engage in more enjoyable activities. She didn't have to work that day, so she had a few hours to herself. She went to the shower, made sure the water was very hot, climbed in, and let it flow down on her head, her shoulders, her back. She stroked her hair, enjoying the feel of the long strands. She hugged her chest. She directed the stream between her legs until she felt the pleasure of release. Then she washed her hair, soaped her body, rinsed, dried off, and went back to her room, trailing the towel behind her.

Ofir wasn't home, and she felt free to walk around naked. She stood opposite the mirror. Water dripped from her hair, and there were still beads of it on her chest. Noa leaned toward the mirror, smiled, and examined her dimples. She turned and looked at her small, tight behind. She rotated and looked at her stomach, pulling it in tight. No, she wasn't thin at all. Maybe she'd be more shapely if she lost a couple of pounds, but she couldn't resist Aunt Farida's delicious food. And maybe she didn't have to. She loved to eat, and she didn't think a woman had to be thin in order to be beautiful. She took pleasure in the full curves of her body. What is going on with me, she wondered. Am I falling in love with myself?

She dressed and walked down the stairs and out into the warm Tel Aviv morning. She strolled confidently through the small, familiar streets, gazing into the colorful shop windows, looking at the faces of the passers-by. She thought about the seminar paper she had to write. She was trying to decide between two subjects, the writings of Yona Wallach and Amos Oz's book *My Michael.* She loved Wallach's poems and admired the poet's intensity; as a result, she knew every detail of Wallach's life. She was leaning toward Wallach and decided to visit *Bet Hasofer*—the literary center that housed every article ever written on Israeli authors. She would look through all the old newspaper clippings and see what she could find. On her way, she passed the used book store. *Maybe I'll pop in and take a look,* she thought, *just for a minute.* She was addicted to these stores; she often found herself buying books, usually poetry translated into Hebrew. She also loved Simone de Beauvoir's books and used to buy them in the English translation. Sometimes she would come across a real find in that unpredictable bookstore, like the collection of an unknown female's poetry from the previous century that had captured her heart.

Noa entered the store, looked up, and gasped. Without realizing it, she took her long hair and draped it over her chest. Across from her stood Ehud, her friend from childhood, the object of fantasies through high school and the army—her first love, painful and unfulfilled. He wore his uniform. It had been a long time since she'd last seen him. When he noticed her, he gave her a look so serious it was almost scary, as though he had just seen a ghost.

"Ehud, what are you doing here?" she said.

"Hi, Noa," he said in a dry tone, "what are *you* doing here?"

"I always come here," she said.

"Um . . . I buy books here, too, from time to time."

"We haven't . . . we haven't seen each other for years," she stammered.

"You're right, it's been years At least five, I think. So how are you, Noa'le?"

I can't believe it, he called me Noa'le. "Fine. You?"

"I'm fine, too." *What a brilliant conversation, so deep and philosophical.*

"What are you up to?" he asked. She was quite sure he had looked at her chest at least twice.

"In general, or now?" she asked.

"Both the former and the latter." *There he goes, still speaking like a soldier.*

"I'm studying and working and living. And you?"

"I'm a career soldier. I left the army to study, then I went back. I serve in the territories, and," he said proudly, smiling for the first time, "I'm already a major."

"Is that what that branch means?" she said, pointing to his insignia and smiling. She wondered what the two of them could possibly have in common.

"Are you married?" she asked, hoping he would say no.

"Not yet." He raised his eyebrows.

"Me neither." She smiled. "Are you here alone?"

"Yes." He didn't elaborate.

She took a deep breath and said, "Do you want to go somewhere? I know a few cafes around here . . . but only if you're in the mood." Her brazenness surprised her.

"I'm meeting someone at the base. Perhaps another time?"

"Okay." Noa looked into his eyes and was overcome by a wave of nostalgia. She remembered why she had fallen in love with him. He was tall and quiet, a born leader. She admired his intelligence, and loved his daring but distant smile. It paralyzed her, that smile, seemed to twist time and space, so much so that at times he seemed to be getting closer and further away at the same time. Noa was desperate for him to stay. She craved him the way an alcoholic craves liquor. If he were to take her in his strong arms and kiss her lips, if he were to stand cheek-to-cheek and whisper that she, Noa, was still his only love, she would have followed him anywhere.

"Well," he said, and the wave of nostalgia washed away. All that remained was a slight tightening in her heart, and the feeling that she had missed out on years of love. "So I think I'll buy this one," he said, pulling a book from the shelf.

"Can I see?" She looked at the cover. "*Things*," she said, "by Yona Wallach. That's such a coincidence. I was just thinking about my seminar paper . . . never mind, it doesn't matter."

"What doesn't matter?"

"Give me the book for a minute. One of my favorite poems is here. Can I read it to you?"

"Why not?" he said, looking at his watch. "I still have a few minutes."

He walks from one edge of my fate
To the other
In a single step
From the edge of the day
In a single step
From the edge of many days
From one edge of years to the other

From one of my edges to the other
From the edge of my light
From my beginning to my end
He walks inside me
From the edge of my body
He sees from one edge of my life
To the other
From my soul to the end of my soul
Knowing me better
Than I could ever know myself.

"Nice," he said, and seemed to mean it.

He's not all superficial, she thought, *there's something deeper there.* "I love this poem. I think it describes a complete love, a love that almost touches God . . ." Noa was shocked to hear herself sharing her philosophy of love with him. Even worse, she was describing what her febrile mind had imagined for many years: that she would find true love, the kind she read about in the poem. All those years, she had imagined Ehud walking from one side of her soul to the other, that it was he who would know her better than she knew herself. She had explained away his reticence, telling herself he was too shy, or that his life was so complicated he never had an opportunity to reveal his true feelings to her.

"That really is a special poem. You've convinced me, I'm getting it," he said. "Okay, I've got to go. I'll see you another time."

"I don't know. Would you want to see me again?"

"Maybe." He sounded impatient. "I really have to go."

"So I'll see you soon," she said.

Ehud didn't respond. He left the store without buying the book. Noa watched him recede into the distance. She stood there, not moving, hoping he would turn around, return and get the book. Perhaps she would have another chance to understand the wild feelings erupting inside her. But he didn't come back, and as soon as he was out of sight, she left and tried to find him among the crowds of people on the street. Noa and Ehud had known each other since their youth group days, and they had served together in the army. He had been her first kiss. She'd been walking him to the midnight bus that would take him to the base, where he would begin his basic training. She thought about that adolescent evening spent kissing and touching each other.

For a long time, Noa had wondered whether or not Ehud loved her, but she didn't dare ask. He never let on about his feelings toward her, whether or not he loved her, whether or not he really desired her. He allowed Noa to love him, sometimes even demanded her attention, but he never spoke about his feelings. Noa learned to be satisfied with what she had and not to ask for more.

With the conclusion of her army service—after her mother had died—Noa returned home to live with her father, and Ehud went on to become an officer. He fought in several battles, and every now and then she'd see his face on television, fighting in the far-off mountains of Lebanon. She had other boyfriends during those years, but none had supplanted Ehud, who remained distant, unattainable, blurry. She grieved for what she had lost. And now, once again, he was leaving without any explanation. No, she wouldn't let him interfere with her good mood. *Each person travels on his own path,* she thought, *each person lives in his own world.* Why didn't he buy the book? Was it because she had thrown him off, or had he never intended to buy it in the first place? She wondered whether her image of Ehud—a gruff exterior enveloping a gentle soul—was real, or whether she had fallen in love with a fictitious character. She smiled to herself and tried to imagine a different ending to their short, strange conversation. And what if they had gone out for coffee? What if they had strolled through the streets of Tel Aviv, or back to her apartment? Would she have met a different Ehud than the one who had lived in her head all those years, or would the same adolescent love erupt within her? And this time, would it be the real thing—mature and mutual? She made her way back to the library. When she got there she asked to see everything about Yona Wallach.

Chapter Ten: Violet

Friday, January 20, 1987

I was born in 1932, in Baghdad, at the foot of the Chidekel River in Iraq. The fourth child of five. My three older siblings, Farcha, Anwar, and Chabiba, were many years older than me. My mother went through a lot before she had me. After me, she gave birth to Farida, and then decided to be content with what she had. All the pregnancies and deliveries had tired her out. Around the time Farida and I were born, my parents became grandparents. I know this sounds odd to people in the 1980s, but in the second half of the last century, it was not unusual. Many women got married right around their twelfth birthday, their Bat Mitzvah, and had their first baby at the age of fifteen.

My mother was considered an odd bird; she didn't marry until the ripe old age of seventeen, and she was nineteen when she became a mother. That's why my nephews were more like brothers to me. You could say that, in certain ways, my mother was a feminist long before the term *feminism* reached Iraq. She started learning Hebrew at a young age, even though she sometimes had to stand on a chair so her teacher could see her. She was the oldest child, and her father made sure she received the same education as a boy. Because my mother's parents had lost a number of children before she was born, my mother was the center of their world. Even after my grandparents had other children, including two sons, she never lost her special place in the family.

My mother chose my father for marriage, which was quite unacceptable at the time. She fell in love with him the first time she saw him, and she asked my grandfather to track him down. My grandfather, who could never refuse his daughter, went out and found my father, who came from a poor and undistinguished family. My father, my grandfather learned, had been supporting his mother ever since his father had returned from World War I, sick and unable to recover. When he died, he left a young widow and her orphan children. My grandfather also learned that although my father had been supporting the family for a number of years, he had still succeeded in becoming a high-ranking civil servant. Grandfather thought that someone like this— upright, strong, hardworking—would be a good match for his cherished daughter. Grandfather loved my father as if he were his own son. He knew my father would always take care of his precious daughter, and he gave the couple his blessing.

Today, when I look back on my parents' marriage, I divide their relationship into two distinct phases: one in Iraq, the other in Israel. In Iraq, bonded by love and a shared destiny, they respected each other. When I was a child, I remember, there was nothing my father wouldn't do for my mother, and she only spoke well of him. All that changed when we moved to Israel. My father lost his status, both as the provider and as an honored member of the community. He lost his property, he couldn't speak the language, and nobody recognized him or his worth. He was simply another new immigrant. He was no longer the person whose opinion and counsel were sought, no longer the person who supported and ran the household. Stripped of his independence and his power, he could no longer control his family, and, as a result, he lost my mother's respect. She mocked him, insulted him, and kicked him out of their bedroom. For many years, his mattress lay in the hallway of our tiny apartment, and none of us were kind to him. Following our mother's lead, we treated him with contempt, which intensified as he grew older and as his behavior changed. Sometimes we saw him strolling on the street with another woman on his arm, and the only time we heard his voice at home was when he shouted in anger. A few weeks before his death, we learned that an orange-sized tumor had grown in his brain. This was what had caused his outbursts. For many years, my heart has been filled with piercing regret at how I behaved toward my father. My mother was the center of our household, the center of my world and the world of my siblings. My father was cast aside, and I never had a chance to tell him I loved him or ask his forgiveness. I cringe every time I remember how I hurt him, and I am overcome with shame for my lack of respect.

But let me return to the subject of marriage in Iraq in the 1930s. In those days, marriages were arranged by the bride's parents, who selected a groom or rejected him based on financial and family status. In our community, we all knew one another, and a family's particulars social, financial, medical were common knowledge. The presence of any physical or mental illness in a family was the most important thing to know. Grandfather understood, however, that in his daughter's case the old model wouldn't work. She was stubborn and opinionated, and if he didn't allow her to choose her own groom, she would never get married. And in the case of my father, Grandfather understood after some investigation that he didn't have to worry. So this untraditional marriage the bride choosing the groom became a reality.

My mother was an independent woman, a socialite who hosted the community's most distinguished members in her elegant home. An invitation from my mother was cause for celebration, because everyone knew she invited only the most important people. She ran her household with a firm hand. We were strictly disciplined, and anyone who angered her paid dearly. This included us, her children, as well as the servants: the wet nurse, the cook, the shoe shiner, the laundress, the driver. If a servant upset my mother in any way, my father would replace him or her that very same day.

My mother did not abide any defiance or lack of discipline, and when we didn't follow the rules, we suffered consequences. I should point out that this policy served us well more than once. None of us died, even though child mortality was very common back then. Her obsessive cleanliness and medical intervention preserved our health and our lives. She made sure we studied, and if Farida and I ever disobeyed her wishes, we were beaten soundly when our father came home from work. *Ima* did not compromise. Everything had to work efficiently and precisely. Anything less was unacceptable.

In retrospect, I think that growing up in Iraq in the forties was wonderful. Elsewhere in the world, there was war; at the time, we didn't realize how bad it was. My father, who learned about World War II via nightly BBC broadcasts, knew that the conflict was spreading, heading our way. To prepare for the inevitable, he stocked provisions for our entire extended family. He collected staples: oil, lentils, and spices, as well as fabric, candles, and anything else he could think of. The war never reached us, but was on the streets of Baghdad: people went hungry, nothing was bought or sold, and there was a shortage of everything. Thanks to my father's vigilance and foresight, however, our family fared well.

In 1940s Iraq, society was organized in a tribal fashion. We lived in a kind of communal house in the desert by the wide Chidekel River. An abundance of palm trees grew on its banks, and we cooled ourselves in its waters during hot summer days. Baghdad, evoked in the songs of Leila Maurad, whose silky voice and forlorn lyrics we loved. Baghdad, where the entire city slept on rooftops during summer. On those hot, enchanted nights, we watched movies in open-air movie theaters. From the rooftops, we looked at the moonlit sky, at the distant, innumerable stars blazing above. On the roof, you could dream about secret, uncharted worlds.

We never felt lonely. We experienced everything together: sadness, joy, hardship, prosperity. If I wanted to spend time alone in the house, I had to wait for months. There were always children to play with: my brothers and sisters, my nephews, the neighborhood children, the children of my parents' friends. We played together, as a group, without a television, of course, or a radio. We invented games, played hopscotch, ball, and leapfrog. We played with dolls. We played for hours—nowhere to rush off to, no extra-curricular activities to attend. There was time for everything; no reason to hurry. We listened to Grandmother Samira—my mother's mother—tell stories about her childhood. We spent time at our neighbor Nezima's house, eating *machbuz*, and we read books that *Aba* gave us. Our world was magical, safe, and carefree.

A world without worries or fear . . . if only I could recapture that feeling. Three years ago, during a routine check-up, I discovered I had endometrial cancer. In the first stage of the illness, I received a number of treatments, including a hysterectomy, which the doctors considered successful. Two years later, I learned the cancer was storming my body, annexing more and more territory. Since then, I've undergone many diverse treatments. I don't sleep much. I lie awake entire nights, reviewing my life, reliving both the beautiful and the excruciating moments. I remember mischief, love, births, and celebrations. I'm unable to work. I haven't gone back to university; I can't focus on my research. It no longer seems important. Nothing matters except for you, my wonderful family. I want to spend as much time with you as possible, to absorb your love, to give you strength. The uncertainty is maddening, even more maddening than despair.

A few days ago, while organizing my desk, I came across some loose pages filled with reminiscences I'd recently written. That's what spurred me to keep a diary. I debated whether or not this was a good idea, but in the end I decided to do it. Life is full of surprises; you never know what the next moment will bring, and there's so much I want to tell you, Noa'le and Guy, and you, too, Dan-Dan. After all, I'm lying here anyway, doing nothing; right now, my whole life is one long waiting period. *What am I waiting for?* I ask myself. So far I haven't find a satisfactory answer. I've been thinking I might want you to know more about me. I've been thinking that you, my dear children, are still so tender. There are many things about my life that I haven't told you about: my childhood in Iraq, moving to Israel, living on a kibbutz, how I met your father, what you were like as babies, my work, and the love I feel for this country. So now, in these long periods of rest between treatments, I am writing to you.

Life unravels so fast, I think to myself, much too fast. People live in bubbles. They think they have an unlimited amount of time. Then something terrible happens that shatters their world, which forces them to contemplate the meaning of life; why we're here; what we're meant to do. They learn to appreciate every moment with their loved ones. Their physical world grows smaller—limited to house and hospital, day after day after day. Normal life ceases to exist, except in dreams. Returning to normal life, to a normal family, is my life's ambition right now. There is nothing I want more than that.

It is unspeakably hard to consider my life today—where I've been, where I'm going. And I'm scared I won't have the time to tell my stories, that you'll never know me as I once was: a mischievous girl, always pushing limits; a young woman, full of dreams, in a magical daze on a kibbutz; a young woman, living in a transit camp with her family, helping to support them; a young woman, steeling herself through *matric* exams, accepted to university, meeting Dan, marrying, giving birth to two incredible, beloved children. I want to tell you about myself.

That's all I can manage today . . . I'll write again tomorrow.

Noa finished the first chapter of her mother's diary. Then she reread it. But she couldn't bring herself to read further. An unfamiliar woman was materializing before her. Aspiring to a normal life? This was a new concept. A strong mother, who doesn't allow anything to bring her down, full of ambition and a love of life: that's who Noa remembered. It was strange to think of her mother as a girl, as a teenager, as a woman in love. She was just *Ima*—that's all. Dreams? Ambitions? Noa wondered what else she would discover. She clutched the diary to her chest for a long time before putting it back under the pillows.

Chapter Eleven: Noa

"Hi, *Aba*! *Shabbat Shalom*! How are you?" Noa greeted her father at the entrance to his house, kissed his two clean-shaven cheeks, and, as she always did, went over to check the pots on the stove.

"I'm fine," Dan Rosen said. "Are you hungry?" He followed her into the kitchen.

"Always," Noa said with a smile, peering into the pots. "What are we eating today?"

"Nothing special. It's just the two of us."

"Where's Guy?"

"He has important business in the middle of nowhere. He went to the *krayot* outside Haifa to see some girl he met on the internet. Enough, Noa, stop eating out of the pots. Let's sit and eat like civilized people," he said, half teasing, half scolding.

"Okay, Okay, but let's eat now. I'm starving," she grumbled. Noa sat at the table, and Dan brought out the food. "Over the internet, you said? That sounds interesting. Now what's going on with you?"

"Slow down, Noa," Dan protested. "I can't keep up with you. Take your plate and let me look at you. You're dressed so nice this evening. What's the occasion?"

"I'm going to a party later."

"I was hoping we could go to a movie together." Dan frowned.

"I'm sorry, *Aba'le*," said Noa. "Listen, I'll try to stop by tomorrow. But I was invited to this party, and Ofir is coming by later to pick me up."

"Oh, fine. I've gotten used to the idea that there are other men competing for your attention." He kissed her cheek.

"Thanks, *Aba*," she said. "You told me over the phone you had something important to tell me. What is it? The suspense is killing me."

"First, eat something. I can see you're hungry. Then we'll talk.

"No. Look, I'm done." She put down her fork and looked at him. "First we talk, then we eat. I'm all ears." She rose from her seat, went into the living room, and sat in her mother's old armchair.

"Whatever you want. You're the boss." He sighed, and sat down opposite her.

"Okay, well, it's like this," he began. "You know that your father is growing up . . ." An ironic smile spread across his face.

"You mean you're getting old . . ."

"You little troublemaker—I'm simply growing up." He rubbed his face with his hands and continued. "In short, I've decided to take a trip in honor of my growing up. You could say that I'm going to find myself. I bought an open ticket to America."

"You're kidding, *Aba*! What's gotten into you?"

"Listen, Noa." Dan tried to explain. "I've been living alone for a long time; I'm tired of my work; I don't want to be two hundred years old and suddenly realize my body is giving out on me, that I can't do any of the things I dreamed about, that it's too late. My boss, Tamir, persuaded me to take a few months off instead of retiring, and I made up my mind to go, and the sooner, the better." Dan breathed heavily; this wasn't easy for him. He knew that Noa would miss him more than anyone. They were particularly close; lately, they'd even been meeting up at the university.

"Wow, *Aba*, you never stop surprising me. Give me a minute, I have to get used to the idea . . . who are you traveling with?"

"I'm traveling by myself. You remember Itzik, my friend from the army? He's been living in Seattle for years. He has a studio apartment downtown that happens to be for rent, and he offered it to me for as long as I want. I'll have a place of my own. This is the perfect opportunity to see the west coast. You can even join me, and we can travel together."

"Sure," Noa said, bitterly.

"Noa, it's not the end of the world." Dan reached for her hand. "I'll only be gone a few months, and it's America, not the moon." He spoke quietly, trying to soften the blow.

"Why do you have to go for such a long time? And what if you decide to stay there? What's so bad about here?" She felt like a little girl again, abandoned by a parent. Her breathing grew ragged.

"It's a little hard to explain," Dan said, staring at the ceiling for a moment before facing her again. "Look, you and Guy are grown. You don't even live here anymore. Do you see? I feel stuck, irrelevant. There are things I haven't done, places I've never seen. I need air, my Noa—I don't want to die without seeing them." He looked into her face. "I want you to be happy for me. Come with me, Noa, my treat. I don't want you to be angry with me."

"What about your studies?" Noa's voice quavered. She felt sadness, yes, but anger, too, even guilt.

"My studies can wait until I come back, Noa'le."

"Everything's always happening so fast," she blurted. "Do you know that I was at Aunt Farida's on Tuesday, and she gave me *Ima*'s diary? You never bothered to tell me it existed."

"She gave you the diary? She didn't say anything to me. And did you read it?" he asked with trepidation.

"I've only read a little," she confessed. "I wasn't up to reading past the first chapter." Her voice shook. "I thought we could talk about it, the diary, but now . . . *Aba*, don't you know how hard it's going to be, not having you here?" She softened as she saw the regret play across his face. Voicing her troubles would make things very hard on him.

Dan made a fist and worked the knuckles against his forehead, as if trying to flatten the creases. "I'm sorry it turned out this way, Noa. She shouldn't have given you the diary yet, at least not without consulting me. It was a mistake, a big mistake."

"Listen," she said. "I understand, you should go . . . of course, you should. I'll be fine."

"You're sure?"

"Yes," she said, faking a smile.

"Now can we eat?" Dan asked as he stood.

"Come, *Aba*." She took his hand. "I need you to know that I want you to be happy. But the distance . . . it's on the other side of the world. I'll miss you."

"I know, my girl, I'll miss you, too. But maybe it'll inspire you . . . to breathe different air, see different landscapes, different people. Now it's my time, and," he said with a wink. "I don't have any grandchildren to take care of . . . at least, not yet."

"I do understand, *Aba*. I'm trying not to be selfish."

He drew her into his arms. "You know you'll always be my little bird. You'll always be in my heart. And if it gets too hard, just hop on the next plane and tour the country with me. It could be really nice. Even the other end of the world is less than a day away."

"Okay."

"Promise?"

"Promise."

"And about the diary, Noa, I'm still here for a bit. If you want, you can read it here, with me. Maybe it's good Farida gave you the diary, even if she should have talked to me first. But that doesn't matter, Noa: Ima wanted you to read it. I think you're ready. It will be good for you to see your mother from an adult perspective. Ima would be very proud of you if she were here." He kissed her head. "And another thing, Noa . . . I love you very much."

"I love you, too, *Aba*," Noa said. His praise had lifted her spirits.

"So can we eat? I'm dying."

"Don't die on me . . . and promise me you'll take care of yourself."

"Always."

"In that case, let's eat," she smiled. "Now tell me, which places are you planning to visit?"

Chapter Twelve: Violet

Sunday, January 22, 1987

When Eddie turned seventeen, he became active in the Zionist movement, and our house became both a meeting place and an arsenal. We had a secret room under the kitchen floor, where we hid the weapons. After the 1941 pogroms in Baghdad, during which Jews were arbitrarily slaughtered on the street, Iraqi Jews resolved not to be easy prey for the Arabs. If there ever was another pogrom, they decided, they would defend themselves.

Right before the declaration of the state of Israel, and especially right after, the plight of the Iraqi Jews deteriorated. People were fired from their jobs, and young men couldn't get into the universities. By the time Jews began to leave, the situation was dire. My parents, along with my brother Anwar and his wife, and Farcha, Habiba, and their husbands, decided to fulfill their dream of living in the holy land and join those who were leaving. There was just one problem: Eddie. When they told him about their plans, he refused to go along; he insisted on staying in Baghdad. As a member of the Resistance, he felt he couldn't leave his friends behind. My mother and Habiba decided that he couldn't be left alone in Iraq; someone would have to remain with him. Eddie was nineteen and mature beyond his years. Habiba and my mother were afraid of what might happen. They knew that if the Iraqis captured any Resistance members, they would torture them until they gave up the names of their comrades, and then the Iraqis would hang them all.

Deciding who would stay behind with Eddie was excruciating, but, of course, it was my mother who decided to make the sacrifice. Eddie was everything to her, and there was no changing her mind. Habiba had small children—her Yosi (called "Yusuf" in Iraq) was only four years old—and *Ima* declared it was Habiba's duty to accompany her family. She swore to Habiba that she wouldn't let him "act out," and that she would be responsible for his fate. And that's exactly what happened: we began making preparations for our move to Israel, with the knowledge that *Ima* and Eddie would remain in Iraq. Farida and I, the oldest of the children, knew what Eddie was doing, and we understood the risks involved. Would we ever see Eddie and *Ima* again? We had no idea.

When *Aba* told us about the trip to Israel, Farida burst into tears. She knew Eddie wouldn't be joining us, and that *Ima* would stay with him. I worried, too, but in other ways I was glad. I was ready for change, for adventure, for something different; I was tired of living in the Jewish ghetto.

We sold what we could. It was forbidden for Jews to take cash out of Iraq, and we weren't about to take any chances. We left most of the money with *Ima* and Eddie. And we still had our house, a huge home with only two people living in it. I insisted on taking my dolls. I was almost nineteen, but I couldn't leave them behind. I'd made them myself, and over the years I'd added new clothes and accessories. They were their own miniature world. *Aba* refused to take the whole collection; he allowed each child to take one thing, no more. I picked Fahima, my oldest and most beloved doll, and I still have her to this day, although she is now in tatters. I can't dispose of her. She is the thread that connects me to my childhood, to my home in Iraq, to the Chidekel River, the palm trees, the desert heat, the aromas . . .

At the airport, I collapsed into *Ima's* arms. I couldn't let go. We both cried, and she promised that she and Eddie would join us as soon as they could. She begged me not to worry. She kissed me through tears and said to take care of *Aba*, never imagining she and Eddie would be trapped in Iraq for over a year.

We wore our best clothes when we climbed into the giant silver bird. We flew to Cyprus, switched planes, and continued to the holy land. When the strange, oversized plane landed, we walked down the ramp and looked around. The heat was the same, just wetter, stickier. I looked for *Aba* but couldn't find him. Then I heard sobbing. There he was, kneeling, kissing the ground and weeping. "*Aba*, why are you crying?" I asked. I was afraid something had happened to him; maybe he had fallen. But all he said, in a trembling voice, was "*Shehechiyanu v'kimanu v'higianu lazman hazeh, amen.*" He was reciting the *shehechiyanu* blessing, thanking God for allowing us to live to see this day. I was a young girl, full of life, and I practically burst out laughing. Then *Aba*

said: "You have no idea how I have prayed for this day,
how I have waited for it, dreamt about it, just like my
father, and his father, and his grandfather. One
generation after another. And I'm the fortunate one. The
day has finally arrived, may God's name be blessed."

I didn't understand. Today, many years after that
moment, many years since *Aba* has passed on, I know
what he meant. He never thought he'd live to see that
day, to touch the land his father, grandfather, and
grandfather's grandfather had wished and prayed for.
And here he was, the first in all those generations
privileged to move to the Promised Land.

Chapter Thirteen: Farida

Farida woke in a good mood. She stretched her legs luxuriously, heaved herself up, and walked over to the closet. It was filled with dresses, some of which she hadn't worn in thirty years, others she'd never worn at all. One of them, a shabby red dress, had been her favorite. Although it didn't exactly flatter the lines of her body, Farida pulled it over her head and examined herself in the mirror. She applied red lipstick, which only emphasized the gap between what she wanted to see and what she did see in the mirror. She slipped on walking shoes, left the house, and headed toward the bus stop. On the way, she encountered Dora, her Romanian neighbor from down the hill, and wished her a good morning.

Dora bombarded Farida with a stream of polite questions. "Good morning to you, too, Farida, how are you? The children? The grandchildren?"

The two of them chatted as usual, Dora complaining about her husband who hadn't left the house since he'd retired, Farida envying her neighbor for having someone at home to keep her company.

"Patience, Dora. Think how nice it is for you, not being alone. I can't remember the last time I woke up next to a man, even one who behaves like a little boy." Farida put her hands on her hips and rebuked her neighbor: "When was the last time someone said something nice to me? Or brought me a cup of tea when I was sick? All my days and nights are like this. Lonely."

"You know what?" Dora chuckled nervously. She seemed taken aback, unsure how to respond to her neighbor of more than thirty years. "You might be right. But believe me, things were better when he was working. At least it was quiet."

"Everything will be alright, Dora," Farida assured her. "You should visit me once in a while. At my house it's quiet. You can have all the rest you want. I'll make you some strong coffee, just as you like it, and we'll read our fortunes in the coffee grounds." They often drank Turkish coffee together, then inverted their cups when they finished, deposited the piled grounds on the table, waited for them to dry, and read their futures in the brown mosaic. "*Ya'allah*," Farida said, trying to wrap up the conversation—it was putting her in a bad mood. "I've got to get moving; my bus is almost here."

"Where are you going?" Dora asked.

"Town. To get my hair cut, colored, and styled. Look at me! I'm a train wreck, as Sigali would say. *Ya'allah*, my dear," she said, "*Salaam*. And come visit me, Okay?"

As she continued down the street, Farida ran into Carmella from the first floor, who asked her about Sigal, and Jamil from the market, who complimented her dress. After that, she felt a little lighter on her feet. She stepped onto the bus, greeted the driver, and sat down behind him.

The bus wove its way through the neighborhood. People came on and got off, said hello to each other, asked after one relative or another. Everyone in the small town knew one another, and they knew all the gossip: who was pregnant and when they were due; who was having an affair; who was getting divorced; who was getting married; who owed money. Knowing each other's business was a fact of life here, for better or for worse, and Farida felt at home. When the bus arrived downtown, she got off and walked toward the beauty shop.

A fellow named Shimon owned and operated the small salon. His uncle had given him the shop when he'd retired. Shimon had renovated the place, installed a stereo system, and installed comfortable chairs. He'd even set up an aquarium for the clients to enjoy. The salon was the social hub of the neighborhood. Everyone stopped by, and not just for a haircut. They came to drink coffee, talk about this and that, see and be seen. Gossip reached the salon first.

Farida walked into the salon, sat down, and gazed into the mirror opposite her. She grimaced as she ran her hand through her hair. Shimon waited patiently for her to complete the ritual, then offered her something to drink.

"Just some cold water," Farida said. "You know how it is, the diet." But when she turned her head and saw the plate of cookies on the table, she was suddenly hungry. She pointed to the sweet date-filled cookies. "Is that *ma'amul*?"

"*Walla*, yes, fresher than fresh. My mother baked them yesterday. Do you want to try one?"

"Your mother, may she live and be well, knows how to bake." Farida took one and tasted it, smacked her lips, and—like a true epicurean—rolled her eyes in pleasure.

Shimon waited for the verdict. "Well? What do you think?"

"*Walla*, these date cookies are the best I've ever had—almost as good as my *baba* with dates. *Ya'allah*, don't be stingy—bring me another one."

"I'm sure you're right," Shimon said. He put the plate in front of her and got to work.

"What are you doing? Are you crazy? I told you I was on a diet. I only asked for one, remember? If you leave them here, I'll eat them all."

"Alright, alright." Shimon chuckled as he removed the plate. He stood next to her, staring at her hair and rubbing his stubbly cheeks. Not shaving—that was the style among young people, she thought, among lazy people. "So what are we doing today?" he asked, passing a comb through Farida's thin hair.

Farida stared into the mirror and sighed. She spoke in her sweetest voice: "Shimon, I'm counting on you. I come in here looking like *kusa machsi*—you know what that is?"

"No, what is it?"

"*Kusa machshi* is stuffed squash. It means I look like what young people call a train wreck."

Shimon was about to respond, but Farida stopped him. "Wait a minute—I still haven't told you how I'm going to look when I walk out of here."

"How are you going to look?" Shimon smiled.

"I'm going to look like a bride," Farida said, tossing her head. "Do whatever you want, *ya'allah*, surprise me." She ran her hand through her hair and flashed him a skeptical smile.

Shimon thought for a minute, then said, "I want to cut the front and the sides and leave it a little longer in the back. And color it. What do you say?"

"Whatever you want, minus a twenty percent discount," Farida laughed.

"It's a deal." Farida was a loyal client, and she also referred a lot of her friends to him.

"Farida," Shimon said. "You know how we do it. I work, and you tell me stories." This was the custom between them. Farida was telling him her life story, one chapter at a time. Every time she went to the salon, Shimon would hear another segment, always with a humorous slant, which he liked.

"So what are we going to hear today?"

"Today you'll hear about what happened when we got to Israel." She said *Israel* with an exaggerated accent. "How does that sound?"

"Sounds good," Shimon said and again offered her coffee or tea.

"You gave me cold water, don't you remember? Listen, Shimon, *I* may be senile, but *you're* still much too young."

"I don't know what's going on with me," Shimon laughed. "You've got me all confused."

"Are you ready to start?" He nodded, and she contemplated Iraq, in the summer of 1950. "Okay. So

111

one day, I remember it was right in the middle of a sweltering Iraqi summer, my father gathered the family and told us they'd decided to move to Israel. I couldn't understand what was so great about Israel; in fact, I thought my life there would be worse. I was angry. I told my father that in Iraq we had friends and family, and I didn't want to leave them.

"My father told me we couldn't go on living in Iraq because we had no money and, regardless, soon everyone would be gone. There was a mass exodus to the holy land underway. You have to understand what it was like back then. My father had been out of work for two years already, but we kids wanted for nothing. Nobody had told us *Aba* had been fired, that he spent every day at the coffee shop playing backgammon. How could I have known he wasn't working? Only on that day did I learn he'd been out of work since Israel had been declared a state. He was fired because he was Jewish, and that was that; he was never able to find another job."

Farida settled herself in the chair. "What can I tell you? It wasn't easy for me to hear that. In my eyes, my father was invincible. He was so strong." Farida made a tight fist. "Eddie, the wunderkind of my sister, *allah yirchama*"—she stopped to wipe away a tear—"the star student of *Shumash*, didn't get into university for the same reason: he was Jewish. He worked as an accountant for a bit and brought in some money, and my brothers-in-law also worked a little here and there. That's how our family got by. You have to understand, they began stripping my father's dignity in Iraq—then, here in Israel, whatever dignity he had left was completely destroyed." Even after all these years, Farida was still angry. "But never mind that—that's a completely different story, the story of my father. Do you know what it means to finish *Shumash* with honors, like Eddie did?"

"What's *Shumash*?"

"It's the best school in Iraq."

"Ah," Shimon said. "Good for him. Those Iraqi bastards."

"Did you know that in Iraq, the whole family lived in a kind of commune?"

"I think I know what you're talking about," Shimon said. "My parents lived like that in Morocco, the entire family together, right?"

"Yes, exactly. Everyone helps everyone else. Remember my nephew, Eddie, who I was just talking about?"

"Yes, of course I remember. You've told me about him many times. He was killed in one of the wars, right?"

"No, not in a war, *allah yirchamu.*" Farida was quiet.

Shimon applied the dye to Farida's hair, not saying a word.

"When my father told us we were moving to Israel," Farida continued, "we understood that my mother and Eddie would stay in Baghdad, because Eddie couldn't leave his friends from the underground. He was a youth leader, too. It broke my heart," Farida said, and even now, forty years after that difficult day, her eyes welled with tears. She wiped more tears from her cheeks. "What can I tell you? I cried a lot that day, and for many days after. I was afraid something would happen, and I didn't want to say goodbye to Eddie, or to my mother. We had to be on the plane within twenty-four hours, they told us. Each of us took one thing, no more, and we wore our best clothes. Can you imagine that? I didn't even have time to get used to the idea."

"That's tough," Shimon agreed. "I need at least a month to prepare for a trip to Eilat."

"On the day of the flight," Farida continued, "my eyes were so swollen it looked like somebody had punched me." She settled her wrinkled hands in her lap. "My father only allowed us one thing to bring, but I brought two, and he didn't say a word. I took two books. One of them Eddie had given me for my fifteenth birthday, a small book of poems by Abu Nuwas, a famous Arabic poet. The other was the Bible I'd received from my grandmother at my Bat Mitzvah. That was it. We all boarded the airplane, leaving the past, heading for a future more different than we could ever have imagined."

Shimon massaged her scalp, working the dye into her hair with his fingers. It felt wonderful.

"The whole flight to Israel, I vomited my brains out," Farida continued. "I threw up and cried. The flying motion made me sick. Since then, I'm telling you, I have never left Israel, not even once." She smiled. "What? What don't I have here? I have desert, I have snow, I have flowers, I have the Kinneret—what else do I need? And when I travel to see those places, I don't throw up . . ." She laughed, but it turned into a paroxysm of coughing. Shimon brought her a large glass of water. She cursed cigarettes and whoever had created them.

Shimon laughed. He rubbed the last application into Farida's scalp, instructed her to wait thirty or forty minutes, and turned to his next client, Ruchama from the bank.

Half an hour later, Shimon checked on Farida. He moved a section of hair to the right, then left, humming while worked. He decided she was ready for rinsing. He told Margo to wash Farida's hair, reminding her to use conditioner. When that was done, he began to cut her hair. Farida enjoyed the touch of Shimon's gentle hands. She watched him work his scissors, watched tufts of her hair fall, hit her shoulders, and drop to the floor. "Shall I continue?" she asked.

"Of course," he said. "*Ya'allah*, please go on."

"We changed planes in Cyprus and finally landed in Israel. I looked around, and what did I see? It was hot, it smelled, everyone was running. It was absolute chaos," she said in disgust. "Someone came and took us to a little building, where they questioned us, asked us our names. Farida, I told them. *What kind of a name is that?* They asked. *That's not an Israeli name. You need to choose an Israeli name, not something funny like Farida. What's Israeli?* I asked. *What's wrong with Farida? Farida is a name from the Diaspora*, they said. Diaspora! Can you believe that?"

115

Shimon looked at her, but Farida didn't wait for a reply: "They changed my sister Violet's name, too, and everyone else in the family. Listen, you'll love this story." Her eyes twinkled. "In Baghdad, our last name was Twaina. My father decided that from that day on, our last name would be Yishayahu Isaiah because he was one of the smartest prophets in the Bible. That was his dream, to move to the holy land and take the name of a prophet. Like it is written in Isaiah, Chapter 62: 'For Zion's sake I will not be silent, and for Jerusalem's sake I will not rest, until her righteousness shines forth like the dawn, and her salvation like a blazing torch.'"

Shimon complimented her on her excellent memory, and she told him that her father, of blessed memory, was religious, and that he'd recited that verse so many times she could recall it in her sleep. Even if she were ensconced in a dream about winning a million shekels in the lottery, she said, she'd be able to recite the line without a mistake. Shimon laughed as he continued to trim her shiny hair.

"Listen, listen to this one," Farida said. "So all of a sudden, I'm not Farida anymore, I'm Shoshana. My sister Violet is Sigalit; Yusuf is Yosi; and so on. Hebrew names, not Diaspora names, that's what they told us."

"So why does everyone call you Farida, and not . . . what was it, Shoshana?" Shimon broke out in a rollicking laugh, making sure to keep his scissors away from Farida's face.

"It's not funny," said Farida, laughing along with him. "Imagine someone coming up to you unannounced and informing you that henceforth your name is Zion. How would that make you feel? Can you imagine?"

"Zion? Why Zion? You're killing me here, Farida. How do you expect me to cut your hair when you keep cracking me up like this?"

"What's so bad about Zion? Haven't you ever heard our national anthem? 'The Land of Zion, Jerusalem?' It happens to be a very nice name." At this point, everyone in the salon was laughing with them. "*Ya'allah*," she scolded him. "Keep cutting. And listen to my story. Maybe you'll learn something about someone else's life. Now, where were we?"

"Shoshana, remember?"

"Yes, of course I remember," she said. "So Shoshana is my Hebrew name, but almost nobody uses it because I don't like it." When nobody responded, she continued. "So after they Hebraicized our names, they loaded us on these trucks, the kind used to carry fruit, and drove us to the immigration office. It was in Atlit, I think. And what do I see? Tents, tents, tents, *ya walli*, rows and rows of tents. I didn't understand what we were doing there, and my father was lugging mattresses all over the place, happy as can be, and my sister was smiling the whole time, and I couldn't stop asking myself, how can this be? I mean, we came from Baghdad, from a comfortable home in a big beautiful city. How did we end up in this hole?"

Shimon and Farida both laughed. "It is a hole, isn't it?" Shimon said.

"Yes," said Farida. "But people came to this hole from Iraq and Romania, and from Morocco, like your parents. Where didn't they come from? And to make matters worse, our neighbors in Atlit were practically on top of us, like this." She clasped her fingers together. "But God save us from the Moroccans."

"Why?" Shimon asked.

"What, don't you know that the Iraqis hate the Moroccans?"

"Really? Why? What did the Moroccans ever do to the Iraqis?" Shimon laughed again.

"You know, I honestly have no idea," she confessed. "But to this day, if you were to ask a genuine Iraqi who his daughter should marry, he would tell you that he doesn't care, as long as he's not Moroccan . . ."

Shimon suppressed a smile and said, "*Walla*, I didn't know that. As it happens, I'm Moroccan, and my girlfriend is Iraqi, and her parents never said a word."

"Then they're bogus Iraqis." Farida sighed. "*Ya'allah*, Shimon, take it easy. I have to catch the bus soon. Otherwise you'll have to entertain me for another hour, and you don't want to do that. *Nu*, it's finally beginning to take shape. It's not bad, this haircut, not bad at all. You should go to England and cut Diana's hair."

"Diana who?"

"Diana who? Diana the princess! Have you seen her haircut? It's from the time of my mother's grandmother!"

"Oh, Farida, Farida, it's so good to see you." Shimon smiled. "You always make me smile, a blessing on your head. God should watch over you."

Farida admired her new hairstyle and hair color, paid for her visit, and left the salon happy. She walked back to the bus stop.

Chapter Fourteen: Violet

Wednesday, February 11, 1987

I, Violet or Sigalit am getting on a strange truck with my family. It's the kind of truck used to carry animals. We start moving. We're all packed in tightly, Farida next to me, little Yusuf now Yosi sitting on my lap. *Aba* sits across from me, dressed in his best white suit; his hands tremble in his lap. We're surrounded by the rest of our extended family. I don't know where they're taking us, and the truth is, I don't care.

"*Ya*, look how beautiful it is here," I say to Farida.

"Beautiful?" she says. "What's so great about this place?"

"Look," I say to her. "You see how the water is being directed toward the trees and flowers? I've never seen anything like it."

"So what?" Farida says. I try to ignore her foul mood. I concentrate on this wonder, which, I later discover, is called a sprinkler. The truck moves on. I'm amazed by all that I see. Unfamiliar trees, people working in the fields, wearing silly hats, waving as we drive by. They look strange to me—they don't wear much: both men and women go topless.

"*Wai, wai,* how beautiful," I say. Every little thing strikes me. It's hot and humid and crowded on the truck, but I could ride for hours, taking in all the sights. I look at my little nephews: couples are sleeping, lulled by the motion of the truck; some look around with wide eyes, taking in the new world. I think how lucky we are to have arrived at this magical place. Farida won't stop sighing. She complains that she can't breathe. I try to calm her, cheer her up; I know this is difficult for her. *Ima* and Eddie aren't with us, and she feels unmoored, adrift. In retrospect, I see she was right. I was clueless. We were in for a lot of hardship. Life would never be the same for any of us.

The truck soon stops, and we disembark. Darkness sneaks in quietly and takes over the street. I look around and see tents, rows and rows of tents. There are loudspeakers, too, in constant use, inundating us with amplified, disembodied voices. I don't understand the messages at first, but later I will learn that they are used for general announcements: meal times, infirmary hours, and so on. I can't imagine why we're here. Maybe we're here to switch trucks?

Then I see *Aba*, my brothers-in-law, and my brother setting up a row of beds on the ground. "What's going on?" I ask my father. "You mean we're staying here? Sleeping in this tent?" *Aba* says we'll be here until they decide where to send us. It seems odd to be sleeping in a tent. We are dressed in our finest clothes, and we have just come from beautiful houses with soft beds. But I don't mind. *What an adventure. Who would have imagined I'd be sleeping in a tent?* I don't dare say this aloud, but my heart beats wildly. It feels like it's the first time I've ever been out in the world, and I'm about to discover its beauty and its grandeur.

"Okay," I say to Farida. "We're here, so why not make the best of it? Let's pretend we're in a golden palace. You see this sand? It's the gold that covers our floors like a carpet, and that piece of cloth waving in the wind is a magnificent regal canopy over our beds. And look, if you peer through the holes in the tent, you can see the sky full of stars, decorating our palace like diamonds. And what fun it is to be sleeping in this palace together!" I manage to coax a smile out of her. Then I push my bed against hers, take her hand, and we both fell asleep.

Farida doesn't think I believe what I'm saying, but that night, my imagination spins out dreams of royalty. I'm glad we're in a tent, in a foreign place. I feel like we've stepped out of the Bible. The tale of the tower of Babel is unfolding right next to me: people are speaking so many different, strange-sounding languages, and you can't tell who comes from where. Unlike the Biblical story, though, which was full of strife and chaos, here we are trying to help each other. We communicate in the universal language of hand signals.

I'm restless throughout the night, writhing in my bed. I hear unfamiliar rumbling sounds. I can't figure out what causes them, and they continue unrelenting throughout the night. The next morning I find out it's the sea. This is the first time I've ever seen it. "*Waii,*" I say to Farida, "look how big it is. You can't see the other side. It dwarfs the biggest river in Baghdad. And it's so blue. What a beautiful sight. What a dream."

Chapter Fifteen: Noa

At precisely ten o'clock, Ofir rang Dan's doorbell. Noa opened the door and grinned at the sight of him. Ofir had made a special effort for Noa instead of dressing in his usual sloppy way, he wore a white shirt and a pristine pair of jeans. His shirt was tucked tightly into his pants, and a brown belt completed his ensemble. Ofir remembered that, in Noa's opinion, the best-dressed men in the world were the ones wearing jeans and a white button-down shirt.

"I'm so glad you came," Noa said, taking his hands. "And right on time, too. Very impressive."

"Hello, Mr. Rosen." Ofir tried to strike a serious, respectful tone.

"Good evening and hello to you, Mr. Ofir," Dan said, shaking his hand. After the obligatory greetings, Dan turned to Ofir and unabashedly asked him, "Where are you taking my princess this evening?"

"Ah, to a geek party."

"Glad to hear it," Dan said, smiling. "Now that I know you're a geek, you can go out with my Noa. If you weren't a geek, I'd be nervous."

Ofir was enjoying the light banter. He told Dan he had nothing to worry about with Ofir himself, but he couldn't vouch for Noa.

Dan, clearly enjoying the conversation as well, told the young couple to have a good time and sent them on their way

"Goodbye, *Aba*," Noa said, embracing her father. "We'll talk tomorrow."

The lights of Tel Aviv lit up the night. Ofir and Noa got into the car. Ofir drove a 1979 Ford Fiesta, which he had lovingly restored himself; they called the car *Dolly*. In recent weeks, Dolly had broken down several times. Ofir had fixed one thing after another. He hoped she would make it all the way to the moshav.

They left Tel Aviv and got on the road to Haifa. The smells of late spring and early summer mingled with that of farms and chicken coops. Noa leaned back, closed her eyes, and breathed deep. She allowed her mind to drift. There was nothing else she would rather be doing than driving endlessly, peacefully, calmly, silently.

Ofir left her to her reverie. They listened to Arik Einstein singing "You." They hummed along with the music, letting the smells, the empty road, the half-moon, and the stars envelope them. Each respected the other's privacy. Noa and Ofir had been roommates for over a year, and they were sensitive to each other's needs. In spite of the challenges of cohabitation, they never argued. They each did what they were supposed to do while trying to make the other person's life as easy as possible.

When they had first moved in, Noa had brought her wide bed, copious clothes, a few books of poetry, her textbooks, and a few stuffed animals she'd had since she was a little girl. Ofir brought a futon, his guitar, and the few clothes and books he owned. They organized the kitchen and the living room together. They bought two second-hand armchairs and used a bright-orange crate for a table. On weekends and holidays, they spread a festive tablecloth over the crate, a housewarming gift from Ofir's mother. On Fridays, Noa adorned the ersatz table with a vase of fresh flowers. They shared kitchenware, some of which had been gifts from relatives, some of it purchased with what little money they had. Every Thursday night—cleaning night—they donned their cheery "uniforms." Ofir wore boxers, and Noa wore shorts and a tank top. They attacked the housecleaning to the accompaniment of rock music, Israeli music, or classical music, depending on their moods. Phil Collins and Sting were particular favorites.

Ofir loved to travel, to have adventures. A physics student, he worked at night and rested during the day. The professors barely knew his name, much less his face; he rarely attended class. Unlike Noa, for whom learning was an integral part of her soul, Ofir simply handed in his work and showed up for exams. The two of them had their own worlds, their own circles of friends, but in the shared apartment, they converged.

The rumble of the engine, the Israeli music, the cold air piercing her lungs, and the quiet presence of Ofir, who understood her so well . . . these things gave Noa a feeling of great tranquility. She thought of the diary tucked beneath her pillow. She thought about whether or not she could talk about it with Guy, if she could ask him over for that very purpose. Maybe she should read it in his presence. She was still wary of her emotions, of the pangs of guilt that tormented her, of the yearning for her mother. Noa tentatively reached over, searching for Ofir's hand. She needed his encouragement, his kind-heartedness, his understanding. Ofir squeezed her hand in return, and after a few minutes turned onto a side street and pulled over.

He looked at Noa and waited to see how she would react. He stroked her hair, trying to figure out what she was feeling. A torrent of emotions flooded his heart. Her vulnerability caught him off-guard. He had always thought of Noa as strong, an optimist, someone who loved life, and this fragility was foreign to him. Noa didn't speak, just curled up in his arms, seeking his body warmth. Ofir held her, guided her head to his chest, and whispered in her ear: "Everything's Okay. I'm here. Why arc you so sad?"

"How come you're always so good to me when I'm so neurotic?" Noa was surprised at her own candor.

"You, neurotic? What makes you say that? Why are you so hard on yourself?" He held her tighter and caressed her back and shoulders.

"I feel so alone, so small in this big world," Noa tried to explain. "I'm so confused; I'm not even sure what's real and what isn't."

"I have no idea what you're talking about, sweetie," Ofir whispered. "Is this about your mother's diary?"

"I'm talking about the fact that the world around me is always changing and, I can't keep up. I'm trying to be independent and strong, but it's hard."

"I still don't really understand," Ofir said, kissing the top of her head.

"Look," sighed Noa. "It's been six years since my mother died, and now her diary turns up, a record I didn't know existed. And then my father decides to go to America. Guy is busy with his own life . . . I barely see him . . . I feel like there is nothing permanent in my life, and that everyone keeps abandoning me."

Ofir was at a loss. What did he, with his modest life experience, know about questions like these? "I didn't know your father was going away," he said.

"Neither did I. Not until this evening, anyway."

"Where is he going?" He stroked her hand and looked into her black eyes.

"He's trying to find himself, acting like he's twenty years old again. First he's going to Seattle, in the northwest part of the United States. From there, he said, he'll travel around the country. He's going to be on the other side of the world—who knows for how long."

"I understand." Ofir took a deep breath. "But why do you feel like there's no stability in your life? It's not like he's leaving for five years, and Guy is around if you need him. And don't forget, I'm here, too. I'm always here. At least, until you get sick of me." He smiled. "I'm right here."

"I know." Noa smiled and rubbed moisture from her eyes. "What would I do without our friendship?"

"I'm sure you would get along just fine without me. On second thought, maybe there is something in what you're saying. It really is hard to get along without me.

It's simply impossible, you know." Ofir wiped a tear from Noa's cheek, and his heart ached. How he wished he could just wipe away this cloud of sadness, just make it disappear. "Noa'le, never forget that you are smart and strong and beautiful and successful."

"Yeah, right," she said, smiling as she pushed him away. "I'm practically perfect."

"I don't get it," Ofir said. "How can you not see it? Look how proud your father is of you. He wouldn't be going away for so long if he thought you couldn't manage without him. And in the end, Guy is always around, even if he's distracted by his own issues. You always seem so together. You look like someone who knows right from wrong, who knows what her goals are, where she's going."

"I wish it were that simple," Noa whispered, "but it's not." She looked into Ofir's face, marveling at the deep blue color of his eyes. And those eyebrows, and the tiny groove in his forehead . . . how could she not have noticed them before? His serious expression touched her. His arms were wrapped around her, and she felt the heat of his body and his breath.

She leaned back, changing her angle of observation. A strange, warm feeling coursed through her. She felt at home, and this confused her: was it only Ofir's friendship she wanted? Or something beyond that? Until that day, she had never thought of Ofir as anything other than a friend, but tonight, with her father's upcoming departure, the wet smell of the earth, the aroma of the orchards . . . something in the air, in the atmosphere, was different.

Ofir suggested they continue on to the party. Noa nodded. Then they were on their way.

Chapter Sixteen: Violet

Sunday, February 15, 1987

When we arrived in Israel, I thought the adjustment would be easy, but it didn't take me long to realize how wrong I was. We lived in a transit camp: Iraqis, Romanians, Moroccans, Hungarians, Poles . . . a host of nations, each with its own customs, language. My family and I, accustomed to a very comfortable life in which servants took care of everything, had to learn to care for ourselves.

And yet, in spite of the hardships, I remember this period quite fondly. I loved the sea, and every day I went to the beach and dug my fingers in the sand, scooping handful after handful. I'd lift my hands and watch the golden grains slip through my fingers. From the moment I laid eyes on the sea, I was drawn to the frothy blue water. I immersed my body, and when the liquid rushed into my mouth, I marveled at its saltiness. In my new country, the sea was my first love, and I love it to this day. It is a salve for my aching body and soul. Whenever I float in the water or lie on the sand, I remember those early days in Israel: the sense of beginning anew, the feeling of hopefulness, the desire "to swallow the entire world right away and all at once!"

At the *Sha'ar Aliyah*—where they processed the immigrants—each tent was given a ration of food. The girls took charge of the situation right away. They watched the small children, and they cooked. Or, I should say, they tried to cook. They had never done this kind of work before, and there wasn't always enough to eat. But we got by. Every morning, the men went to work. My father's job was to help pave the roads. On his first day, *Aba* wore his best white suit. He didn't realize he'd be doing physical labor rather than sitting in an office, like he had in Baghdad. The next day, he wore different clothes.

Aba—who'd been a valued employee of the Iraqi government—didn't complain. Not then, not ever. Every day, right up until he died, he thanked God for bringing him to the holy land, even after *Ima* arrived and the family dynamics shifted so dramatically.

The little kids were unfazed by the colorful tapestry of cultures. They played together from the start: Romanians with Iraqis, Russians with Poles. They all looked alike. They communicated with the very basic Hebrew they all had. The only thing that distinguished the newcomers from all other children, who arrived earlier or from the native Israelis, the "Sabra" kids, was their clothing. The Israeli children were, in my opinion, the most beautiful I had ever seen: tanned skin, sparkling eyes, short pants, sunhats, confident smiles. That was my first impression of these children, called "sabras," I later learned.

At the *Sha'ar Aliyah* they taught us a smattering of Hebrew, but, for the most part, we communicated in sign language, usually accompanied by laughter. I recall one time—I wanted to ask for an egg. No matter how hard I tried, I couldn't remember how to say *egg* in Hebrew, so I clucked like a chicken and put my hand beneath my rear end, hoping someone would see I was mimicking a hen laying an egg. At first, our Romanian neighbor had no idea what I was asking for, and the two of us erupted in laughter. She called her son, who immediately understood: he was sure I wanted a chicken.

This was a time of uncertainty. Every day, trucks brought new immigrants and trucks transported other immigrants from the *Sha'ar Aliyah* to different parts of the country. We waited our turn like everyone else. We never imagined we would ultimately be separated from everyone else: from *Aba*, from our brothers and sisters, from our beloved nephews.

After a month at the *Sha'ar Aliyah*, the adults in our family were gathered and informed that *Aba* was going to an *Ulpan* to learn Hebrew, after which he would do government works. The rest of us would be scattered among the various kibbutzim willing to take us. My brother and his family were going to one kibbutz, Farida and I to another. We were classified as adults so that we could support ourselves and stay together. I was almost nineteen, and Farida was nearly seventeen; we'd need to round her age up a few years for her to be considered an adult. My older sisters were sent to two other kibbutzim.

We wept as we boarded separate trucks. We'd never been apart from one another, and the prospect was terrifying.

Farida refused to be comforted. I promised her she and I would never part. I swore on my life, and on *Ima's*, and on our grandfather Reuven's (our mother's father, beloved by both of us). "I will never leave you," I told her. "That's how it's always been, and that's how it will always be." I hugged her, stroked her hair, held her to my heart. Today, I think of how I may leave her forever, sooner than I'd imagined. To this day, I have always been at her side, through everything, and I will remain so until my last breath. She is a part of me, flesh of my flesh, my beloved sister, my soul's twin . . .

For Farida, the move was agonizing. First, she'd had to leave *Ima* and her beloved Eddie. When we got to Israel, her material comforts were gone. Now she was leaving *Aba* and Chabiba, Anwar, and Farcha. For my part, I wasn't particularly distressed, despite all the goodbyes. Israel had cast its spell upon me: the smell of the sea filled my nostrils, and the Carmel Mountains tugged at my heart. Every day, I was greeted by the sight of the Carmel, in all its glory. So green, so proud. I loved the diversity of my neighbors; I loved hearing the many languages. These people were so different from those I had known before, and, yet, quite similar, too.

The pine trees bowed their heads, as if welcoming me to their land. Time seemed arrested. I felt I could go on like this forever, driving between the mountains. The path was twisted, and the road was narrow. We had to stop so other drivers travelling in the opposite direction could pass us, but I didn't care. I knew Farida and I were together, that it was going to be wonderful. Farida calmed down, and for the rest of the ride, the two of us sat in silence. Lost in her own thoughts, she eventually fell asleep. I cradled her head in the crook of my arm and stroked her hair. "Don't worry," I whispered. "Everything will be alright."

Chapter Seventeen: Noa

That night, Noa dreamed of Ehud. In her dream, he hurried to an urgent and covert mission, and he called to ask for her help. He wanted to know if she could pack thirty-eight sandwiches, for the unit, and a few bags of fruit. She agreed immediately and got down to work. She crossed the street near her parents' house and headed to Avram's market, where she purchased ten loaves of bread, big salami, and much humus. Avram asked her what all the food was for, and she told him it was for her brother's birthday; she couldn't reveal the truth because she'd promised Ehud to keep the mission a secret. Noa paid and returned home. When she returned to her parents' house, her mother asked why she'd bought so much bread. Noa didn't answer for a moment. Then she composed herself and explained she was preparing care packages for the soldiers. Her mother returned to her study. She was writing an important article, she told Noa. If Noa needed help, she knew where to find her.

Noa went to the kitchen and began slicing bread. As she prepared the sandwiches, she imagined Ehud's lips touching the bread she was handling. She cut two slices, spread humus on them, pressed them together, and wrapped the sandwich in brown paper. She imagined Ehud's hands unwrapping the paper, bringing the bread to his mouth, lustfully biting off a hunk. His teeth would grind it up, his tongue would lick the humus, and he would swallow the whole thing, one bite after another.

His saliva would soften the bread, his tongue would roll it around in his mouth, his teeth would crush it, and his belly would absorb the warm dough. Noa wondered whether he'd be thinking of her while he ate. Then, suddenly, she was standing, naked, in front of piles and piles of bread.

She prepared stacks upon stacks of sandwiches; the task was endless. Ehud devoured one sandwich after another: egg, cheese, mayonnaise, humus. The stacks grew taller and taller. Noa wiped her brow, and Ehud stood opposite her, angry, intimidating. Why hadn't she completed her assignment? Did she want the entire operation to fail? He had to go, and nothing was ready! She thought, *don't leave me again*, but didn't say it. She made another sandwich, then another, and suddenly, instead of Ehud, it was a Gestapo officer towering over her, holding a whip and cursing. Again, the sandwiches piled up in gigantic heaps, hundreds of them, thousands, sandwiches of every imaginable kind. More and more and more, and soon the room was full of sandwiches, there was no room for her, she was being crushed to death.

Noa woke in a panic and ran to the bathroom to vomit. When her stomach was empty, she leaned back, her breath coming in short, staccato gasps. A bad dream, she told herself, a nightmare. No doubt spurred by her chance encounter with him that morning and because of everything that had happened in the last few days. Between her mother's diary and her new-found feelings for Ofir, no wonder she was disoriented.

Ofir approached her sleepily. "Hey. Are you okay?"

She nodded. "Sorry if I woke you. I must have eaten something at the party that didn't agree with me."

"You barely ate anything," Ofir said. "But boy did you drink! You must have quite a mixed cocktail there in your stomach." Ofir reached for Noa's hand and kissed it lightly. "Come," he said, leading her to the bathroom sink to wash her face. Noa allowed him to do as he wished, as if she were a little girl; the feeling was pleasurable. Her mind was clear. She felt safe, and she knew Ofir would take good care of her, that she would be alright. He pulled her close and kissed her on the lips.

"No," Noa whispered, turning her head away.

"Why?"

"Because my mouth must smell terrible," she stammered.

"Your mouth happens to smell very sweet," he said, inhaling her scent.

Noa turned to face him. She wrapped her arms around his neck and looked into his eyes.

"I want you," he whispered.

"I want you, too."

"Now?"

"Now."

Ofir pulled her close, very gently, as if she were a crystal doll. He hugged her. Noa put her cheek next to his and breathed deeply. Her heart beat fast.

"It's been a long time," he said.

"What's been a long time?"

"I've wanted you for a long time, but I didn't have the nerve to do anything about it. Tonight, in the car, I almost swallowed you up, but I restrained myself. Just."

Silence.

"I've been waiting patiently," Ofir went on. "Waiting for you to want me back." He looked away, embarrassed at his candor.

"Why didn't you say anything? Why did you remain silent all this time?"

"I was afraid."

"Of what?"

"You."

Noa took him by the hand and led him to her room, pulled him onto her bed. She folded down the blanket and looked into his eyes. Then, biting her lips, she began taking off her clothes, one item at a time, letting him take in her movements, the curves of her increasingly exposed body. Noa sat at the edge of the bed and pulled Ofir close. "Tonight we don't have to dream," she whispered in his ear. "Tonight our dreams become reality."

Chapter Eighteen: Farida

Farida woke in the middle of the night with a throbbing headache and couldn't fall back asleep. Once again, Eddie had haunted her dreams. In her dream, Eddie reached up from under the ground, and she tried to pull him to safety. He struggled, but the more he fought, the deeper he sank. He stretched his arms toward Farida, begged her to rescue him. He was fifteen again, maybe sixteen, and his gorgeous green eyes looked her right in the face. Farida taunted him. *Pull yourself out of the swamp,* she said. As if he had chosen to go in. She looked at him with disgust, the way one might regard a smelly child. *You could be my grandson by now,* she said. She told him the train was long gone. She continued to laugh at him, at his weakness. Eddie kept pleading for help, to keep him from drowning, but this made her laugh harder. She walked away, but Eddie's desperate cries followed her. She ran, but his voice grew louder, and Farida awakened, sopping in sweat.

She heaved herself out of bed and breathed deeply. "Just a dream," she told herself, "it was just a dream." She tried to quiet her pounding heart. She went to the bathroom to urinate; according to Iraqi lore, urinating acted like a reverse vaccine, rendering all bad dreams powerless. "Eddie," she whispered. "*Allah yirchamak,* Eddie. God have mercy on both of us. Oh . . ." She splashed water on her face, again and again, but still couldn't quiet her mind. She struggled into her tattered bathrobe, grabbed a box of cigarettes, and stumbled to the sunroom. She lowered herself into an armchair and smoked one cigarette after another, waiting for the new day to begin. It seemed to take forever.

She looked out the window, at the street. An occasional car passed, but not a single soul ventured by on foot. Sliding her feet into her slippers, she sighed deeply, then limped back into the kitchen.

She opened the cabinet and took out a *finjan* to make coffee. She put in a spoonful of freshly ground coffee it smelled of cardamom and added a generous amount of sugar. She filled a small mug with water from the tap and tossed it into the *finjan*. She turned the burner on low, placed the pot on the flame, and stirred. The coffee and sugar combined, and a light froth began to form. Farida slipped into her past: forlorn memories of unfulfilled love and a shattered heart.

Like the coffee percolating in the *finjan*, her memories of Eddie were both bitter and sweet. She remembered the first time they were separated: she had moved to Israel, and Eddie, unwilling to abandon his fellow Resistance fighters, had stayed behind. She remembered, too, their passionate reunion after so many long months, and the stories of his dramatic escape to Israel—stories that seemed part "Tales of the Arabian Knights" and part a TV espionage series.

"Eddie," she murmured. "Eddie." In Iraq they had almost hanged him, and later on, in Israel, war had killed him for good. People say time salves wounds, but Eddie's absence still burned in her heart. Her widowhood and loneliness only intensified her longing. She still remembered his face. She still heard his voice. He was her first thought when she opened her eyes in the morning, and at night, his mischievous smile was the last thing she saw before she fell asleep. Every night she reminded him and herself that one day she would join him, and they would finally be together forever.

Chapter Nineteen: Violet

Friday, February 27, 1987

Evening fell. From a distance, we could see the newly built villages. Small houses poked up from the treeless hills, like new teeth in a baby's mouth; they were a soothing, pleasing sight. Some of the mountains were barren, but if you looked carefully, you could see a few pine trees through the fog. Lights flickered in the darkness, visible from miles away. As the bus wove its way through the twisted roads, I played a little game of hide-and-seek with myself, trying to predict when the next lights would appear. Groups of short, squat houses continued to dot the hills kibbutzim or Arab villages, I later learned. By the time we arrived, it was dark. The bus inched its way to the kibbutz gate.

"Wake up, Farida," I whispered. "We're here."

Farida stretched and rubbed her eyes. "We're here?"

"Look," I said, "we're about to enter our new kibbutz."

"Why are we just sitting here?" Farida asked, sweeping her arms across the landscape.

"I don't know," I said, looking around.

We heard the driver talking to the kibbutz security guard.

Every part of my body ached. My sister had been sleeping on my shoulder through the entire ride, and I couldn't wait for her to get up. Finally, the guard opened the gate and we drove in. I saw little trees on both sides of the road and, beyond them, small houses. After a short drive, the bus came to a stop next to a larger building the dining room, I found out later.

A heavyset woman welcomed us. She smiled broadly, pointed to herself, and said, "Miriam." She did this for our benefit; the majority of passengers on our bus had come straight from the *Sha'ar Aliyah* and knew only a few Hebrew words. Farida and I knew a bit more, because our mother had taught us in Iraq. Miriam acted like a Super-Mother: there was no limit to the number of children she could accommodate. Many of them were even younger than Farida and me. Twelve- and thirteen-year-olds, separated from their families. There was room for all of us in Miriam's generous heart, and I liked her from the moment I saw her. I knew she would relieve me of some of the burden I felt, worrying about Farida. I sensed she would support me, help me. For the first time in a long while, I felt a semblance of peace; we had finally reached a place we could call home.

Miriam assigned us rooms and handed us work clothes. I looked at the garments, then at Farida, and the two of us burst out laughing. When leaving Iraq, we'd packed our best dresses, the ones *Ima's* seamstress had made for us. But nobody could have been happier than I was that day on the kibbutz, trading in my fancy dress for loose-fitting work clothes. Later, when looking in the mirror, I realized the short pants accentuated the curves of my body and that between the buttons of my shirt people could catch a glimpse of my breasts. I shoved my hands in the pockets of my shorts, and Miriam took us

143

for a short walk around the kibbutz. From that day, the only time I ever removed those clothes was on Friday nights, when we'd shower and put on the simplest dresses we could find. Here on the kibbutz, those dresses looked like they'd come right out of a fashion magazine.

I loved walking in the Kibbutz pathways in the evenings, especially on those Shabbat nights which were very special on the kibbutz. Seeing the other families walking out in their best clothes was a thrill: men and boys wore khaki pants and shirts, and women and girls wore dresses, skirts, or even pants, which in those days was very unusual. When I saw them making their way to the dining room for our weekly Shabbat meal, my heart ached. I'd look at Farida, and see my feelings reflected in her eyes, her expression full of longing. Oh, how we yearned for our family, scattered throughout the Middle East. *Aba* would visit us from time to time, but we rarely saw the rest of our family. Most of all, we longed for *Ima* and Eddie.

That first night, our tour of the kibbutz took us past brightly lit houses, the dining room, the laundry (which was completely new to us), and the dormitory where we would sleep. Farida and I stepped into our new room and exchanged gratified smiles. We'd been living in a tent for a month, and now, finally, we were back in a real room, with four walls, a small closet, and a window looking out on an orchard. Next door lived two young men, Holocaust survivors from Poland. At first we were shocked at the thought of living next to men, but our discomfort was short-lived. We instantly found a way to communicate with them, primarily through primitive sign language that sometimes left us in hysterics. We kept this up until we'd all learned Hebrew.

I will never forget our Hebrew classes. The older I get, the more ridiculous they seem. Our language teacher at the kibbutz was an old, bald man with a thick German accent; he believed using the works of our national poet Chaim Nachman Bialik was the best way to teach us. Poems like *Gather Me Under Your Wing, and Be for Me both Mother and Sister* were our texts. He had decided to teach us a highbrow, poetic version of Hebrew. Rather than teaching us the language of everyday conversation which is what we really needed— he used a refined lexicon culled from the poems of Bialik. We paid the price for this every time we spoke to native Israelis, particularly children, who stared at us when we spoke, as if we were a bunch of circus animals.

The cultural gap between us the new immigrants and the Sabras was huge, but much goodwill existed on both sides, and a feeling of solidarity asserted itself and enabled us to overcome the challenges. I remember many funny incidents that highlighted the differences between both groups. One time, for example, I sat in the dining room eating rice with a spoon, as we had in Iraq. An Israeli man sitting across the table looked at me in bewilderment. "If you eat your rice with a spoon," he chided, "you must drink your soup with a fork." It had either not occurred to this gentleman that people from different places have different customs, that what is considered acceptable in one society is not acceptable in another, or he was having fun at my expense. I hoped the former but feared the latter.

More than once, the linguistic challenges made me smile. I remember one time, working in the kitchen, when I asked another worker to pass me the *matanah* the gift when what I really wanted was the *matateh* the broom to sweep the kitchen floor. She didn't understand, of course, until I pointed to the broom. Laughing, she said, "*Matateh*. Say it: *matateh*. That's what you want, right?" She looked at another worker and rolled her eyes. "What a concept, like it's a real gift to sweep up the kibbutz dining room." It was embarrassing I felt like a little girl but I learned the difference between the two words, and I never made that mistake again. For a long time after that incident, everyone referred to the broom as "the gift," completely befuddling the newcomers. The broom-gift had become an inside joke, shared by all who worked with us.

Chapter Twenty: Noa

Late in the afternoon, Noa awoke from a deep sleep. A single, piercing ray of sunlight blinded her. She lifted her heavy head and looked around. She had a nasty headache. She dropped her head back onto the pillow and sighed. A large, warm hand caressed her brow, and for a moment she panicked: she didn't know whose hand it was. She felt warm breath on her neck, and then someone kissed her. She remembered the previous night's events and blushed.

"Good morning," Ofir whispered.

"To you, too." She turned to him and smiled.

"Did you sleep well?"

"It was a black sleep do you know what I mean?" She gazed into Ofir's face and was struck by his handsomeness. His eyes kind, blue, familiar watched her, and his unruly hair grazed his bare shoulders.

"My head kills," said Noa.

"No wonder, after all you drank yesterday. But don't even think of telling me that last night happened because you were drunk." He smiled.

"Of course that's what I'm telling you." She returned his smile then haughtily turned her back on him.

"If that's the case," he said, "then I know exactly what to do to get you to sleep with me."

"You wicked man," she whispered. "On the other hand, I can always pretend I'm drunk so you'll take advantage of my vulnerable state." She pulled him close and kissed him.

"So either way, you're not responsible?" He was enjoying this.

"Never." Pleased with herself, Noa pushed her face between Ofir's warm hands. "Would you mind bringing me a cup of coffee and an aspirin?"

"I'll promise you half my kingdom if we can spend the rest of the day in bed."

"Sounds good," Noa said, pulling away from him, "but unfortunately I have to work on my seminar paper."

"What's it about?"

Noa sat up. "I'm writing about Yona Wallach, and it's an absolute nightmare finding any written material about her. I'm really breaking new ground."

"That sounds interesting," said Ofir, "very creative."

"Yona Wallach's personality fascinates me," Noa said, forgetting about her headache for a moment. She's brave and provocative, just a fabulous poet. I suppose I admire her."

"From what I know about Yona Wallach's poetry which isn't much it seems to me that you can love her or hate her, but you can't ignore her. I'd say she's a little crazy," Ofir said, giving Noa a sidelong glance. "What is it about her you love so much? Is it her provocative personality or her wild and complicated poems?"

Noa considered Ofir. He had strong opinions about many topics outside physics, his area of expertise topics that, by his own admission, he knew little about. But he was smart, and while he might not intimately know a given subject, he usually made trenchant observations. She found their discussions interesting and challenging.

She told him that if she wanted to answer his question properly she would have to research every aspect of Wallach's work and life, but the more she understood about the poet, the more mystified she became. She'd begun by focusing on Wallach's creative use of language, but now, studying her in the context of feminist theory, what she really admired was the woman's courage. Wallach was willing to test all limits. She had no boundaries—not with sex or sexuality, nor with words. She did not distinguish between literary language and street talk. No Israeli poet had ever done this before.

Ofir looked at Noa with amusement and admiration. He was touched by her enthusiasm, by her eagerness to prove to him that this poet who had insinuated herself into Noa's heart was in fact worthy of her respect, and maybe of his respect as well. He stroked her hair and told her that having this kind of conversation so early in the morning made him hungry. He admired her fighting spirit, he said, even when her head was pounding.

Noa gazed at Ofir's naked behind as he climbed out of bed. She stretched and smiled with contentment as he walked into the kitchen to make coffee. The sun shined outside, and her pillow was soft. She heard Ofir in the kitchen, opening cupboards and running water, and inhaled the wonderful smell of fresh salad and fried eggs. This morning, life seemed beautiful. A few minutes later, Ofir returned, grinning, with a large tray loaded with a luscious breakfast and two aspirin. How was it that all this time, she hadn't been able to see him as a sensual man? And what was it that caused the relationship to change so dramatically? And how could friendship blossom into something bordering on love? And what was love, anyway? Did she even know the meaning of the word? She felt unsettled and, to her astonishment, her eyes filled with tears.

There were times, in the past, when Noa had thought she knew what love was. With Ehud, she thought it was the real thing, but in fact it was a one-sided, frustrating, painful kind of relationship. She and Barak had seemed to experience a genuine love but, in retrospect, it was selfish and all-consuming, something she'd seized on to help her through the difficult period after her mother died. She'd been dependent on this love, until realizing she couldn't rightfully call it her own. She'd been *in* love, but she knew she still hadn't gotten to the heart of the matter.

She thanked Ofir for the splendid breakfast, and for his attention and friendship. "Why don't you sit here next to me," she said, "and I'll feed you. One bite for me, one for you." Noa offered a forkful of food, then another. With each bite, he kissed her knuckles.

Noa savored both the attention and the reciprocity. She felt strong, alive, and full of optimism.

When they finished eating, Ofir drew her close, caressed her face, and whispered into her ear. He told her she was the one. That he'd loved her from the moment they met. He told her about the day he'd replied to her advertisement at the university: how he'd climbed to the third floor and rang the bell, how the sight of her dried his throat, how her long black hair, dark eyes, and luminous face bewitched him. He had decided, on the spot, to share the apartment, and ever since that day, nearly two years ago, he had been waiting for her. He didn't dare take the first step until he knew she was open to love; he waited until she was ready to love him back. He couldn't believe he was telling her this, he whispered.

Noa sat on the bed and listened, smiling to herself. Her legs were drawn up, her arms rested on her knees, and her head lay on her forearms. She told him she'd been drawn to him, too, from the moment she saw him, but she'd never thought they'd be anything more than friends. She said she was touched, and very happy, but he needed to be patient, because she still felt confused.

The color drained from Ofir's face. In the past, women had fallen in love with him easily, but not so with Noa. Nevertheless, he had assumed, after their passionate night together, that Noa would feel as he did.

She took his hand, pressed it to her heart, and looked him in the eye. She told him he was her best friend in the world. That everything was still so new, he had to be patient. She wasn't emotionally prepared for what had happened last night, and, as lovely as it had been, she still needed time.

"Best friend in the world," Ofir said. "I hope you don't mean best buddy."

"I don't mean best buddy," Noa replied with a smile. After a moment, he told her he thought he understood what she was trying to say—or at least he hoped he understood. He hoped she didn't consider last night a momentary lapse or an exploited opportunity, but she assured him it had been mutual and that, with time, everything would be clear.

Ofir pulled her close again, and tucked a loose strand of hair behind her ear. "I have all the time you need," he whispered, "and all the patience. I'll wait for you forever."

Chapter Twenty-One: Violet

Monday, February 16, 1987

I just finished another grueling round of treatment. Most of my hair has fallen out; I gather the remaining hair into what I call a "savings-and-loan" hairdo, on account of its attempts to make a little bit look like a lot. Then I cover it up with a wig that I bought in B'nei Brak. It's awful. My beautiful hair.

I lie in bed for days at a time, exhausted. I stare at the ceiling and I wait, not knowing exactly what it is I'm waiting for. Sometimes I imagine I'm a captured princess and that at any minute my knight will come and carry me far, far away. Then I pull myself together and smile weakly. Who could possibly save me from myself? It is my own malevolent body holding me prisoner. I feel like someone sentenced to a lifetime of hard labor: he comes home at the end of the day, lies down in his berth, and stares hopelessly at the ceiling. All of his limbs throb, and he knows that the next day, and the day after that, and all the days after that, will be just as tortuous, and he doesn't know what to pray for—that tomorrow will arrive quickly or not at all.

And if it weren't for Dan—my dearest friend, my rock—and for our wonderful children who look after me, whose happiness, I know, is dependent upon my happiness—if it weren't for them, I would have given up long ago. But you are my beloved, my safety net. You are my princes and princesses. It is for you that I battle this cursed disease, and it is for you that I write. I have to bear witness. What started out as a mission—to tell you about my past, to share my life with you—has turned into a sanctuary, a warm and welcoming reprieve from my suffering. Writing frees me; it feels good to remember the past. My life was rich and beautiful, and I have no regrets. And so, back to Eddie, my incredible nephew. There has never been anyone quite like him, and there will never be.

Eddie stayed in Iraq with my mother, and the house continued to serve as headquarters for the Resistance. During the day, Eddie supported *Ima* and himself by working as a junior accountant at a haberdashery; his boss was a Muslim willing to hire Jews. At night he worked with the Resistance, performing military exercises both inside the house and on the streets of the Jewish neighborhoods. They wanted to be sure that there were no disturbances where they lived, that nobody was plotting against them from within.

The prevailing mood had it that Jews were responsible for Baghdad's problems. If a person didn't get a job, it was because "the Jews took all the positions." The same was true if someone didn't get accepted to school. If the cost of housing went up, or if it went down, or if there was any kind of shortage, it was always the fault of the Jews. Our family had had enough of the hatred, and we knew that at our first opportunity we would leave this country and go to the land we'd dreamed of, the land of our fathers, our eternal home. And we did.

Most of those who left Iraq moved to the Holy Land. There were some who tried their luck in other places, usually following in the footsteps of a relative who'd sent them tickets and money, but the vast majority went to Israel. The land we had dreamed about for so many generations could now become real. Every Passover, for countless years, the Jews of Baghdad had greeted each other with the words *next year in Jerusalem*, and now they could actually fulfill the quest and move their families to the nascent state. People left everything and just took off. Most couldn't even take money. They exchanged lovely homes and warm beds for a life of austerity and hardship. Their tents were leaky in the winter and sweltering in the summer. Their days were exhausting, and their new homeland was fighting for survival. But regardless of the cost, they finally had a home of their own. Most paid the price with love and never regretted it.

And so the number of Jews in Iraq dwindled each week. Both my grandfathers, along with my maternal grandmother, passed away in Iraq. My other grandmother, Daisy, moved to Israel shortly after we did; my uncles and aunts were already there; our close friends, too. Muslims were moving into what had been the Jewish neighborhoods, and there was a feeling of insecurity. Eddie never considered leaving his friends. He was confident no harm would befall him. And *Ima* she opened her home to the whole group. Aside from Evelyn, our one non-Jewish servant, the household help had moved to Israel. *Ima* had to learn to take care of the house by herself. If it had been up to her, she would have gone with the others, but she had promised my sister Chabiba that she would take care of Eddie. She would protect him, she said, as if he was a rare gem, and she kept her word.

For the first time, *Ima* did all the cooking and the cleaning. Eddie's friends came over every evening. Evelyn helped, but since *Ima* couldn't pay her, Evelyn worked mostly in other people's homes. If possible, she would have moved to Israel with the rest of us.

Every so often, *Ima* would implore Eddie to leave Iraq. His response was always the same: "I have a responsibility to those who are still here. As long as they're here, I'm not going anywhere."

Ima waited for weeks, then months, for Eddie to agree to go. As the Jewish community grew smaller, her longing for the rest of us intensified. She was tired of this unsettled life, tired of the constant worrying. But Eddie showed no signs of wavering. In fact, as more of his comrades left for Israel, his role in the movement became more crucial. He worked to smuggle his friends out of the country before the Iraqis could catch and hang them in the town square. Sometimes, while waiting for the next flight out of Baghdad, they took refuge in *Ima's* house.

Ima soon realized that Eddie had no intention of leaving. At first she tried persuading him, appealing to his conscience: "Your mother is going crazy," she told him. "She doesn't sleep at night, doesn't eat during the day it's hell for her. There's nothing here for us anymore. What if something happens to you? How will I be able to look your mother in the eye? What about your father, and your brothers? and what about Farida and Violet? Don't you miss them?"

But Eddie was intractable. He continued to tell my mother that he had a responsibility, and he couldn't walk away from his friends. It would just be a little longer, he said. Only a few more people had to leave. How could he even consider abandoning his confederates in a place like this? *Ima* waited. As time passed, she sank deeper and deeper into despair. The noose was tightening, she felt, and if she didn't get them out soon, they would both hang from the same gallows, like other Jews, many of whom they'd known. One morning *Ima* woke and knew she couldn't continue living this way. She had to do something, now, before it was too late. It was time for her to stop him from putting both their lives at risk, and that's exactly what she did.

Chapter Twenty-Two: Farida

Early the next morning, Farida awakened to the sound of the telephone ringing. She struggled from her armchair and shuffled to the phone. *I suppose I did fall asleep after all,* she thought to herself.

"*Ima?*"

"Sigi? Why are you calling so early? Is everything alright?"

"Everything's fine," Sigi said. "But I need to ask you a favor. Ruthie didn't feel well last night, and I don't want her in school today."

"A blessing on her head, my soul, may God watch over her. What does she have?" Farida ran a hand across her face.

"Don't get so upset, *Ima*. It's really nothing. She has a little fever, that's all. Listen, I have to get to work, I have an 8:00 meeting. I'm dropping her off at your house, okay? Can you be downstairs in twenty minutes?"

"A blessing on your head. Of course, bring her over?"

Sigal thanked her mother, and Farida began putting the house in order. She washed coffee dregs out of the mugs and opened the blinds and windows to air out the house. The smell of cigarettes lingered, but a pleasant breeze blew through the small apartment.

Farida took some *machbuz* out of the freezer and put them on a plate decorated with white flowers, a plate Ruthie adored. Then she went to the bathroom and put in her false teeth. She dressed, combed her hair, and looked at her reflection in the mirror. "*Ya walli,*" Farida muttered. "An old lady . . . it is what it is, every day a little older . . . and those wrinkles . . . ." Sometimes she couldn't find herself in the lines of the face looking back at her. She left the apartment.

Farida sat on the stone fence outside the building and waited for Sigal. She imagined she wasn't a wizened old woman, but a young lady waiting for her suitor. She looked at everything familiar to her: the bus that came by at precisely 7:15, the children reluctantly walking to school with bags slung over their shoulders, the grocer stacking milk cartons and bringing in fresh rolls.

She looked at the sun, basked in its warmth, enjoyed the wonderful morning nature had bestowed upon her. She spotted Sigal's car and straightened her clothes, leaned forward, and wrapped her arms around herself, as if her granddaughter were already standing there. When the car stopped, Ruthie jumped out and ran into her grandmother's arms. Sigal said goodbye and went on her way. Farida held her granddaughter's small hand, looked into her innocent face, and wondered how such a tiny creature could be the source of so much happiness.

"Okay, Tutti. What should we do today?" she said with a wide smile.

"Whatever you want," the little one answered.

"You know what, let's go upstairs first, have something to eat, something to drink, and then we can go for a little walk." Farida kissed Ruthie's forehead. "I see your fever has gone down." Farida ruffled Ruthie's hair. "A lot of new flowers have blossomed in the field across the way. And there are a lot of stories for me to tell."

"Hooray, Safta! That's what I love more than anything else in the world." Ruthie smiled and looked into her grandmother's eyes. She took Farida's wrinkled hands in her own and gave them a tiny squeeze. Ruthie's small hands couldn't cover the spotted, calloused hands of her grandmother, but Farida felt their touch keenly, and a sense of fulfillment, joy and purpose filled her.

The two of them walked upstairs: one in the dawn of her life, young and innocent, inexperienced, and the other in her twilight, seeing the world with clear open eyes, counting her days, trying not to think about the impending sunset. This day was a gift for them both: Farida would inhale the sweetness and bustling joy of youth, and Ruthie would reap the fruit of her grandmother's experience, wisdom, and unlimited generosity.

Chapter Twenty-Three: Violet

Sunday, March 1, 1987

Spring is in the air, and I, too, feel myself coming back to life. The blossoming of the almond trees and the smell of citrus awaken me, lure me outside. Yesterday Danny took me to Sidney Ali beach in Herziliya. We wanted to see the poppies peeking from underground, enjoy the view of my beloved sea, bask in its salty air. Guy has gone on a field trip with his class for a few days. Noa's in the army. And we, the young couple, are free to do as we wish.

Guy has a new hobby: photography. Right now, I am his subject, and he chases me around the house night and day, photographing me from every possible angle. I get out of bed, he takes a picture. When he follows me to the bathroom, I have to laugh. That's it, I say, enough! There are some places even he is not permitted to go. Guy sits and waits patiently for me to get out of the shower, then surprises me again. Sometimes it can be irritating, but I try to encourage him. He is talented, and if this is what he needs in order to learn, so be it.

When we drive, Danny holds the steering wheel with one hand and squeezes my hand with the other. Sometimes he brings my hand to his lips and kisses it. I get very emotional. Even now, after all these years, romance triumphs over all. I feel Danny's love and devotion, and I am afraid. I am afraid of two diametrically opposed things. On the one hand, I'm scared that if I don't win this battle against cancer, Danny's sadness will break him. I often tell him that if something does happen to me, I want him to build a new life for himself, but he always cuts me off and changes the subject. On the other hand, I'm afraid that he *will* build a new life for himself and forget me. I know this isn't a reasonable fear, that the children will always remind him of me, but jealousy and possessiveness still assault me, driving me to the brink of insanity.

I am besieged by painful feelings. I am afraid of leaving Danny, and I fear the loneliness he will experience when I'm gone. I feel guilty, too: for being so possessive, so inconsiderate, so insensitive, for wanting to be the one and only woman in his life. It simply isn't possible. Maybe these thoughts are natural, who knows? I don't dare say a word to him about my feelings. Why hurt him? But being able to put these thoughts on paper is very therapeutic. It puts my mind in order and liberates me from the distress that weighs upon me.

Never love another,
Never take her hand on an autumn night
Or whisper words of love in her ear

This is part of a poem I wrote many years ago; these words resonate in my tormented mind. To be his forever. A popular Israeli folk song runs through my head: "You and I will change the world." I hum the tune to myself, and my frustration turns to rage. Not only did we not change the world, but it's gaining on us every day, controlling our lives, turning them upside-down without any warning. Fate tricks us, and laughs its bitter laugh.

When we arrived at the Sidney Ali beach, we gazed down at the water. Normally, we would have approached the water's edge and hiked among the ruins, but yesterday I was too weak. This place brings back so many memories: Shabbat mornings with the kids, long walks along the shore, breathtaking sunsets. Little things, tiny moments of contentment imprinted on my heart. My eyes filled with tears, and Danny ran over to hug me.

This morning, the house is quiet. Even Danny's not here. This is a good opportunity to write about *Ima* and Eddie's immigration to Israel. I return to the spring of 1951. In the end, after waiting for many long months, *Ima* finally understood that she couldn't wait for Eddie to decide. She couldn't count on him to make the necessary arrangements for their *Aliyah*. It was clear to *Ima* that time was short, and the longer they waited, the more dangerous it would be. She decided to take action.

One has to understand: Eddie was young and fervent, an uncompromising idealist. He had lost all perspective. From a meek and undistinguished member of the Resistance, he'd risen to a high-ranking officer, and he believed it was his duty to stay until the end. And so *Ima*, who knew it was up to her to initiate the process, started investigating different avenues. She learned that the Resistance oversaw the *Aliyah* process. In order to move to Israel, the first thing she'd have to do was renounce their Iraqi citizenship. She knew that if she wanted to keep this from Eddie, she would have to go to a city where the concept of *Aliyah* didn't exist. *Ima* asked her servant, Evelyn, to speak to her relatives in Hili. After Evelyn confirmed there was no formal *Aliyah* activity in that city, *Ima* decided to try her luck there. She would go to Hili, and quietly renounce their citizenship. If Eddie figured out what she was doing, she knew, all was lost.

This was right before the spring holiday of *Shavuot*. In Iraq, we referred to this holiday as "Visitor's Day" because Iraqi Jews had a custom on this day of visiting the burial places of the pious. They would prostrate themselves upon the graves of Ezra the Scribe, near Chara, and Ezekiel the Prophet, in the village of Chifel, right outside Hili. *Ima* left a note for Eddie saying she was going to the cemetery in Chifel to pray for her family's welfare, and she'd be back the following evening. Eddie thought it a bit odd, since his grandmother was not particularly religious, but he was very busy and ignored his misgivings.

Ima left the house early the next morning, taking a small pocketbook and a lot of money for bribes, to ensure the immigration process would be quick, efficient, and discreet. She stuffed the money into her bra and wrapped herself in a big black shawl, like an Arab woman. All that could be seen were her two coal-black eyes. She climbed into a carriage and rode to the train station.

Aromas at the bustling train station aroused her senses. The morning smell of *chubiz,* a kind of Iraqi bread, filled her nostrils. Peddlers sold their wares, people were pushing, being pushed. Even at this early hour, the heat was oppressive. *Ima* bought a ticket and strode toward the train; she looked for Evelyn, who was going to accompany her on the journey. The faithful servant waited next to the train. She was flustered: she and Mrs. Twaina would take the train together! It wasn't every day someone of her standing had the opportunity to travel with such a distinguished woman. Not only would they spend several hours with each other, but Mrs. Twaina, because this was a secret mission, planned to spend the night with Evelyn's family!

The two women boarded the train, crowding inside with everyone else. They walked through one car after another, and when it was clear there were no seats available, they stood in a corner. *Ima* stared at a male passenger, and he stood and offered his seat. In those days, men were gallant toward women of high social status. When I remember those days, I feel sick to my stomach: the concept of one person being worth more than another never sat well with me. My mother, on the other hand, never altered her worldview, and even in her death, many years later, she thought of herself as a queen stepping down from her throne.

Ima sat the entire time, while Evelyn stood next to her, fanning the noblewoman's face. I heard later that my mother did not stop complaining about the heat and the stench, and it never occurred to her to let Evelyn rest her feet, not even for a few minutes. And Evelyn stood there, shielding her from the heat and the pickpockets, tending to her. Years later, I encountered Evelyn on a busy street in Ramat Gan, a suburb of Tel Aviv largely populated by Iraqis. She smiled when she told me about their long train ride. When she talked about my mother, her eyes shone with admiration. I was uneasy: in the young, idealistic state of Israel, the concept of class didn't exist. I thanked her for being so devoted to our family for so many years, but I felt awkward with guilt.

After a long journey, they finally arrived at Evelyn's family's home in Hili. There, too, my mother was treated like royalty. In honor of her visit, the hosts had cleaned and scoured, cooked and baked, even given up their bedroom. *Ima* accepted their hospitality with equanimity; after all, wasn't a woman of her status entitled to such treatment?

The next day, the two women set out at dawn. They went to the municipality, where *Ima* filled out forms for renouncing citizenship; she had to forge Eddie's signature. After their citizenship was annulled, she submitted her request for a visa to Israel. In exchange for a small bribe, she was able to get the right forms that same day. Usually the process of moving to another country took weeks, or even months, but to *Ima's* good fortune, the combination of her charm and money moved things along. From there, the two women took the train to Chifel, where they prostrated themselves at the prophet's grave.

Ima prayed for a long time, asking God to bless our family. That was the last time any relative of ours visited the cemetery. It's been over four decades since then, and who knows how many more years will pass before someone from our family visits the prophet's grave. After their visit, *Ima* and Evelyn caught the train back to Baghdad. A few days later, *Ima* and Eddie boarded a plane that took them to Israel, to their family. *Ima* never could have imagined the two formidable challenges of her life: First, getting out of Iraq, second and much more difficult spending the rest of her life in Israel. A life that was about to change forever.

Chapter Twenty-Four: Noa

The weekend passed pleasantly for Noa and Ofir. On Saturday afternoon, Noa's brother Guy stopped by. He came through the front door, vaulted onto the living room sofa, put his hand on his belly, and said, "Is there anything to eat around here? I'm dying of hunger."

"Of course," Noa said, smiling. "Have you forgotten I'm half Iraqi?"

"What? You, too?" Guy laughed.

"Come into the kitchen; we'll make something. I have to talk to you anyway." Noa took his arm and pulled him off the couch.

"Hi Guy, bye Guy," Ofir said. "I hate to run, but I'm working the night shift, and I can't be late." He turned to Noa. "I'll call you later."

"Bye." Noa ran her finger along his cheek and walked him to the door.

"Hi and bye to you, too," Guy said. "May we meet only on happy occasions."

"Amen," Ofir said, and he closed the door behind him.

"What was that all about?" Guy asked.

"What exactly do you mean?" Noa couldn't help smiling.

"Is there something going on between the two of you?"

"What makes you think that?"

"Hi, bye," he said, mimicking Noa's voice. "All lovey-dovey. What's happening, big sister? Is this what you wanted to talk to me about?"

Noa blushed. "At this point there's nothing to say. But he is cute, isn't he?"

"I'm sensing my older sister is trying to hide something from me. Fine, I understand. But I'll just say this: I wouldn't object to having Ofir as my brother-in-law. He has a good head on his shoulders."

"My lord, you are so far off. It's really not what you think. But enough of that. What do you want to eat?"

"I don't care, just make me something already." Guy sat down at the cluttered kitchen table. "So what's going on?"

"Everything's fine. What do you think about *Aba's* plans?"

"Actually, I think that going on a trip will do him good. Clear his head a little. Most people see the world after the army. *Aba's* doing it in his retirement. I think I understand him. You know how life can be one big pressure cooker? Especially after what he went through those last years with *Ima*. He deserves some relaxation."

"And you don't mind if he goes?" Noa's voice was hesitant.

"Not at all. I'm happy for him. He's given so much of himself let the man live a little!"

"I know you're right," Noa said. "And I'm ashamed to say this, but I feel like a little girl whose father is abandoning her."

"Noa, what's gotten into you? Nobody's abandoning you." Guy tilted his chair back and gathered crumbs into little piles. "He's going for what, a few months? Don't make a big deal out of it. Anyway, I'm here for you, and as I see from the look in your eyes, so is Ofir." Guy smiled knowingly. "You'll be fine. Remember, you're not a little girl anymore. So, what's with the food? I'm on the verge of rummaging through your garbage can."

"Calm down, would you?" Noa chuckled. "Here some first-aid." She handed him a peeled cucumber. "Yes, I know I'm not a little girl. Everyone's always reminding me of that. Isn't it ever hard for you? Don't you ever miss people?"

"You mean *Ima?*"

"Yes, *Ima*, for example."

"I've gotten used to her absence. Not that I never think of her," he added with a mouth full of food.

"So don't you think it'll be hard having *Aba* gone, too?"

"Of course I'll miss him, but I'm also happy for him. I wish you felt the same way."

"So what are you saying that I'm being childish and selfish?" She averted her eyes.

"Noa, I wasn't trying to say anything like that. I just want you to be happy for him. Just try not to upset him. Don't make him feel like he's abandoning you."

"What? did he say something to you?"

"He hinted that he was thinking of chucking the whole idea because he didn't want you to feel like he, too, was leaving you."

"That wasn't what I meant." Tears started in her eyes, and she angrily wiped them away. "It's just a little hard for me."

"I understand what you're saying." Guy took a huge bite of the omelet she had given him. "But you have to support him, send him on his way. He deserves to live a little bit, too."

"You're right." Noa looked down. "You're right. Sometimes I feel like you're the older one, not the other way around. Where do you get all this maturity from?"

"From life." Guy smiled broadly. "From life, Noa'le. It's time for you to grow up. Anyway, where's my sandwich?"

"Here," she said, putting another plate in front of him. She leaned back, and for awhile neither spoke. Guy ate with gusto, and Noa admired her brother's hearty appetite. They were both immersed in their own thoughts, their own memories, their own worlds.

"Look," said Noa after a bit. "I think you're right we'll be fine. *Aba* should go. And like you said, we've got each other."

"Exactly," said Guy. "That's exactly what I'm saying. I'm not going anywhere . . . for the time being." Guy smiled wickedly. "Anyway, anything else you wanted to talk to me about? Because for a few days now, I've had a feeling there's something on your mind, something more serious than *Aba's* trip. Wow," he said, licking his fingers, "that was a good sandwich."

"Thank you." She sat down across from him. "There was something else I wanted to talk to you about. Or more accurately, tell you. I don't know if *Aba* had a chance to say anything."

"What didn't he tell me this time?" Guy asked. "I'm always the last one in the family to know."

"So I assume you don't know I visited Aunt Farida this past week and that she gave me *Ima's* diary?"

"What diary?" He seemed genuinely surprised.

"It seems *Ima* kept a diary."

"When did you say you visited her?" Guy asked.

"A few days ago."

"And you're only telling me now?"

"I wanted to tell you yesterday, but you didn't go to *Aba's*."

"And what about the day before that?"

"Relax. I had a crazy week. Anyway, that's not what matters right now."

"Of course it matters! I'm sick of this. Nobody bothers to tell me anything." His voice was angry, but there was a slight smile on his face. "And anyway, why now? And why did she have it in the first place?"

Noa tried to strike the right *older sister* tone. "First of all, if you want people to tell you things," she said, "you might want to try asking. As for the diary, Aunt Farida said she felt I was ready. *Aba* gave it to her, maybe because she was so lonely, maybe for some other reason, I'm not really sure."

"Did they want me to read it, too? You know what, it doesn't matter," Guy said, shaking his head. "Where is it, anyway?"

"In my room."

"So go get it!"

"Slow down a minute!" Noa was taken aback. "Let me say something."

"Why? Is it full of secrets?" Guy looked into her eyes.

"I don't think there are any secrets, but I haven't gotten very far. I can say the diary is loaded."

"What do you mean?

"It's loaded, with details, with information about her family."

"That's what it's about?" Guy was visibly disappointed. "What is it, a history book?"

"No." Noa smiled. "You'll see. But listen. I'm not giving it to you until I've finished it. And one more thing."

"What?"

"I just want you to know that it feels very strange to me, reading what she wrote. At first, I was afraid to even open the book."

"Afraid? Of what? Did you think some evil spirit would leap out? You know what, Noa? I'm a doer. I don't think about things too much, I just do them. What do you think—the journal's going to bite you? You're whittling your life away, Noa, thinking too much and doing too little. My God," he said, "the way you complicate everything."

"I'm not afraid of any spirits." Noa chuckled. "And maybe I do have a tendency to complicate things. But I didn't know what to expect, and I didn't know how it would affect me. I kept it under my pillow for two days. By day three, I couldn't contain myself anymore, and I started flipping through it, a page here, a page there. It really touched a nerve. Just seeing her handwriting got me choked up." Noa looked down. "It reminded me of when we were kids, how she used to sit in her room for hours, working on her science publications."

"So you didn't actually read what she wrote?" Guy said. "And *Aba* knows Farida gave you the diary?"

"*Aba* knows. I talked to him about it. But not too much," she added quickly. "I asked him why it took so long for us to get it. Turns out he agreed with Aunt Farida. Didn't think we should read it until we were ripe, as he put it."

"Ripe, huh," Guy said. "What are we, potatoes?"

"No, but I do think they had our best interests in mind. And it wasn't easy talking to him about it. I was too flustered to ask any personal questions, especially now that he's leaving. And I didn't want him withdrawing into his own world again." Noa leaned her elbows on the kitchen table, took a deep breath, and continued: "In a way, the diary brings *Ima* back to life. He spent such a long time mourning her I didn't want to open all that up again."

Guy nodded. "But you know what? It still kills me he didn't tell us about it in the first place."

"I was angry, too, at first. But I think he just thought we were too young, that not enough time had passed since her death."

"Maybe it *is* still too soon. Maybe I should ask *Aba* if reading it will traumatize me for life," he said quietly. "*Ya'allah*, go get the diary. At least let me see it."

Noa went to her room. She still kept the diary under her pillow. She picked it up and ran a hand over the cover; it was thick, hard, and unadorned. She stroked the book as if it was an actual part of her mother, as if it was a hand extended from another place, another time, another world. As she walked back into the kitchen, she dropped the diary. It hit the floor and opened, pages spreading out like a fan. As she picked it up, she noticed a loose page, protruding from between two latter pages of the diary. She pulled it out and realized it was a letter, addressed to both Guy and her, written in her father's handwriting.

My dearest Guy and Noa,

Now that you are reading your mother's diary, you are already mature, self-sufficient adults. I am sure you will be moved, as I was, when you read through these pages. They are full of Ima's thoughts and memories; they describe her life as she experienced it. I believe that reading this book will be a thrilling and enriching adventure for you; inside it, you will find an entire world. You'll be amazed to discover that although children think they know their parents very well, sometimes they are only familiar with one facet of their mother or father. A whole life can be hidden from their eyes. You have been very lucky, my children, that Ima kept a diary, primarily for you. The diary was written with love. Ima wanted to bequeath to you the story of her heritage, her family, and the love she felt toward you. She knew she wasn't going to be with us for very long. This diary will allow you to see Ima from other vantage points, to know her in other ways, to share her experiences, the ones you know about as well as the ones you don't.

When I think about the way I experienced my parents, it seems to me that in each stage of my life, I related to them in a different way. As a child, I worshipped them. They were invincible. I depended on them for everything, and I experienced the world through their eyes. I will never forget the way you were in this stage of your lives, how you wanted to be like Ima and me, how you mimicked our behavior. This was the best time for our family. Dozens of images pass before my eyes: I remember Noa standing behind Ima, watching her get dressed for a night out; I think Noa must have been six or seven years old. You told Ima that soon you would have breasts, and that when you did, you'd be able to study with her at the university. I remember you, Guy, sneaking up behind me while I was shaving, asking me to dab some shaving cream onto your face because you already had an enormous mustache. I think you were about four, but whatever age you were, you certainly didn't have a mustache.

As you grew, my sweet children, the revolution broke out: adolescence. This was accompanied by the painful realization that Ima and I whom you had idolized were not omnipotent. We were just people, and we had weaknesses and deficits. It hurt me to see the disappointment in your eyes. Not only were Ima and I not omnipotent, as you had once believed, or at least hoped, but we were inconsistent. Sometimes we were strong, sometimes weak, sometimes terribly fragile. Ima's illness and death made our fragility and our impermanence strikingly real, but that's life. I want it to be absolutely clear to you that Ima never gave up her fight against cancer, not for one minute. It's just that the cancer overpowered her. She had no choice.

When you become parents yourselves, my children, you'll start to see more and more parallels between the parents who raised you and the parents you've become. I think it will be easier for you to see Ima and me as we really are: flesh and blood, with strengths and weaknesses. The rebellious stage will be over, and you the children/parents will have a new appreciation for us, your parents, who raised you and cared for you and allowed you to become parents yourselves. And most likely, the cycle will continue.

A circle is closed when our parents, who raised us, start depending on us. As our parents age, they look to us, their grown children, for support. We hold them up, we protect them; the cycle changes direction. And the world turns, and a generation is born, and a generation dies out. The rules of the world don't change except for when tragedy strikes, as it did in our family. I ache at the thought of your premature adulthood, at how you had to watch Ima suffer, and worse, how you lost her at such a young age. Ima tried so hard to shield you from her pain. She didn't want you to grow old at such a young age. But she couldn't protect you completely—you saw, and felt, her pain. You are good people. Ima and I must have done something right. I am proud of you, and I love you.

Aba

Noa didn't tell Guy how she longed for her mother, not that night or for many nights to come. But Noa felt she needed her mother more than ever. Finding and reading the diary made her yearn for an earlier time, when she lived with both of her parents and her younger brother, safe and protected. Back when she had a real family. Her father's postscript had given her new insight into her own world and its vicissitudes. "Ima," she whispered to the diary. "Take care of us."

Chapter Twenty-Five: Violet

*P*urim is in three days; I can dress as a cancer victim. I'm already bald. I just hope the little kids aren't scared of me. Usually *Purim* is a very festive day for our family, but this year, Noa's staying at the base and Guy is too old to dress up. Anyway, he doesn't care about family celebrations. Apparently he's at the age where he has no interest in anything. It is what it is. Every year we gather at my older sister Chabiba's house, which is as large and spacious as her heart. She loves to have everyone over. We are, thank God, a gigantic family, and between weddings and births we get bigger every year. If only I could be privileged to hold my own grandson or granddaughter in my arms. Oh, my dear children. How I want to accompany you on the road ahead, how I pray for the strength and the good fortune to stay in this world and experience all these moments with you.

When my father, of blessed memory, was still alive when you were little he had his own *Purim* tradition. He would give all of his grandchildren, big or small, newly minted coins or bills that he brought straight from the bank. By now, all of you have a respectable collection; I wonder if they're worth anything? When my parents were still alive, we would dress up and celebrate *Purim* at their house, in their tiny slice of backyard. Children and adults surprised each other with original costumes. We spread a rug over the grass, sat down, and took turns presenting our costumes in the most creative way we could. We put on skits, sang songs, and danced while Anwar's daughter Adena played the accordion.

Back in Iraq, our *Purim* celebrations were full of laughter and good cheer. Everyone had a chance to show off his or her natural talent. Chabiba prepared her special *Purim* pastry cheese pastries, *sambusk, ka'kaat,* which is like a small pretzel, and of course *baba* with dates. She also made *zangula,* a kind of honey-dipped pastry, sweet marzipans in all sorts of designs, and many other desserts. Other family members brought their own talents, too: we played musical instruments, sang songs, told stories, put on plays.

Farcha's two sons, who are only one year apart, put on the funniest plays. There was always a healthy competition between the two boys, but they have always been close, in both age and character. One brother would tell a story while the other stood behind him and wrapped his arms around the storyteller's chest, his hands gesturing wildly in accordance with the story. He would tie his brother's shoelaces, adjust his brother's pants, put his hands into his brother's pockets, light a cigarette and put it between his brother's lips whatever action the story called for. The two of them had a real flair for drama, and we were always rolling on the floor. Today they are both mature adults, but sometimes, if we ask very nicely, they'll relent and perform for us again.

Our *Purim* celebrations in Israel were different. We didn't dress up, but we marked the holiday in other ways. The table was always piled high with delicacies, like in Iraq. We went to synagogue dressed in our finest clothes. We waited all year, us kids, for the reading of the *megillah*. Every time the evil Haman's name was recited, we shook our noisemakers and screamed, making as much racket as possible. This was nothing like other visits to synagogue. Usually were on our best behavior, sitting quietly and respectfully. *Purim* was the one day of the year we were allowed to act out, make mischief, and be as silly as possible. The novelty never wore off, and every *Purim* we were as excited as ever.

Since coming to Israel, we rarely go to synagogue. Moving here took us further away from religion and closer to "Israeliness." The only person who continued to attend services was my father. He went to synagogue every morning and kept the traditions until his dying day.

Aba was thankful for all that God had given him. He was especially grateful God had granted him the privilege of coming to the Holy Land, of living there, raising his family there. On the anniversary of *Aba*'s death, the whole family gathers at his old synagogue to honor his memory. Perhaps we do it to appease our own consciences: we'd stopped treating him with respect from the moment we first arrived in Israel.

Chapter Twenty-Six: Farida

In the early afternoon, Farida took her little granddaughter Ruthie for a show off walk through the neighborhood. It's the kind of walk that's very popular in neighborhoods like Farida's, where everyone knows everyone else. As you promenade, you show off your little treasure, and before your eyes, every silly little thing she ever did or said is transformed into a brilliant accomplishment. Whenever Ruthie asked a clever question, or remembered one of their names, or identified a flower, or gave someone a compliment, the neighbors were astounded. How she's grown, they would say. How beautiful she is (like her grandmother), how clever she is (like her great-aunt, of blessed memory), how she lights up the whole town with her joy (also like Aunt Violet, of blessed memory). And could it be she looks like Noa, Violet's girl?

In the hallway, they bumped into Chaimke, who patted Ruthie on the head, greeted the two of them, and asked why the little girl wasn't in school that day. They answered, at the same time, that Ruthie was sick. Then they both almost laughed but restrained themselves, not wanting to embarrass him. Chaimke looked away, implying this kind of buffoonery was beneath him. He muttered something about how he didn't mean to be rude, but he was in a rush, then he moved quickly down the stairs. Farida and Ruthie stepped aside to let him pass, and the moment he was out of sight they burst out laughing while trying to keep their voices down. When they reached the first floor, they knocked on Carmella's door. An Iraqi immigrant like Farida, Carmella was delighted to see them and immediately began heaping blessings upon Ruthie.

"A blessing on your head, Ruthie, may you be protected from the evil eye how you have grown!" Carmella spat to both sides of the girl, wrapped her arms around Ruthie, and smothered her cheeks with kisses. "She looks just like you, Farida you're like two drops of water," she announced, clapping her hands. For several minutes she continued to bless and spit, bless and spit; then she urged pastries upon them and begged them come and spend some time with her. Farida gracefully declined; they couldn't stay, she said, because she had promised to take Ruthie for a walk through the wildflowers across the way. Another time, thank you, goodbye. They took their leave and continued down the street to Dora's house.

Dora's house, which was always immaculate, was filled with the aromas of cooking and baking. Dora and Aaron were childless, and Dora invested all her energy in preparing food for her husband and anyone in the neighborhood who might need help. Whenever a woman had a baby, Dora visited the same day with all kinds of food. If someone was sick, God forbid, she appeared on their doorstep with steaming pots in her arms. Dora loved to feed people, and people loved to eat her food. Giving to others helped ward off the loneliness she sometimes felt. In exchange for her generosity, her neighbors made it their business to invite her and Aaron for Shabbat and holidays.

Before they entered Dora's home, Farida made sure to remind Ruthie not to ask about Dora and Aaron's children. "They have none," she pronounced. "End of story."

"Of course they have children," Ruthie said. "Dora's always telling me they'll be back any minute, but no matter how long I wait, I never get to meet them." She looked skeptical. Whom should she believe, Dora or her grandmother? Because she couldn't decide, she continued searching for an answer she could accept once and for all.

"Dora doesn't like those kinds of questions. She has no children, Ruthie," Farida said, "so stop asking her about them. It puts me in a very uncomfortable position, do you understand?"

"But why don't they have children?" Ruthie asked, for the hundredth time.

"Because some people just don't have children. Dora couldn't have children—that's why they don't have any. Okay?" Farida was losing patience.

Ruthie persisted. "Why couldn't she have children?"

"Because that's how life is. Enough with the questions, Ruthie." Farida ruffled her granddaughter's hair. "Just do what I say. Don't ask about children."

Ruthie shrugged but didn't promise anything. She knew she wouldn't be able to keep her word if she did. Dora greeted them warmly and invited them inside.

"Come in, come in. Welcome. What are you doing, standing there in the doorway?"

"We just came by to say hello," Farida said. "We're on our way to the field. The flowers are magnificent this year." Ignoring her friend completely, Dora lifted Ruthie in her arms, as if she were an infant and not a second-grader.

"Aaron," she called to her husband, "you're never going to believe who's here. Sigali's girl Ruthie! Come. Come see this little doll." Aaron came in and began his interrogation. "What, there's no school today? What's your teacher doing without you? Who's your best friend at school? How much is seven plus seven minus seven plus seven?"

Farida could tell that Ruthie enjoyed being the center of attention. She answered all the questions willingly, looking at her grandmother from time to time and smiling. When she got mixed up, she simply corrected herself and went on, which pleased her hosts even more. After finishing Dora's ice-cold lemonade, Farida and Ruthie wound up their visit and headed for the door. At that moment, Ruthie couldn't stop herself.

"When are your children coming home?"

Farida looked at her granddaughter in embarrassment and wrinkled her eyebrows, trying in vain to signal Ruthie to change the subject.

"They're not here today, my dear," Dora answered. She looked at Farida in desperation.

"So where are they?" After stealing a quick glance at her grandmother's cringing face, Ruthie looked directly at Dora, her eyes pleading for answers. *Let them tell me the truth just this once,* she thought, *and I'll never ask again. Maybe I'll finally know whether or not Dora has children. If she doesn't, why not? And if she does, where are they? And how come whenever I visit Dora and Aaron, the children aren't home?*

"They went on a long trip," Dora answered sadly.

"And you don't miss them?" asked Ruthie.

"Yes . . . yes, of course I miss them," Dora said.

"We really ought to get going," said Farida. "Soon it will be too hot for us outside." She put an arm around Ruthie's shoulders and propelled her toward the door. "The winter was so difficult and the summer will no doubt be very hot, so we have to take advantage of this beautiful day." Farida spoke quickly. "There's been much rain this year thank God the Sea of Galilee is full and there's enough water. Maybe this year, for a change, they won't ask us not to water our gardens. I can't stand dry grass; it's just a reminder of death." Sweat sprung out all over her body as she tried to undo the damage. "It's really very sad to see it, and whenever I see grass that hasn't been watered in a long time, and it's starting to turn yellow, I have this urge to turn on all the sprinklers and let the poor thirsty grass drink to its heart's content."

Dora smiled. She nodded to her friend, covertly thanking her for once again rescuing her from the young girl's relentless questions. Farida hoped that because the girl was so sweet and Farida's granddaughter

Dora might not be offended. They'd known each other for many years.

"I remember when your mother was born," Dora said to Ruthie. "Moshe was on reserve duty, there was a war, so Aaron and I took Farida to the hospital."

"And two day later, at five in the morning," said Farida, "I knocked on your bedroom window and said, 'Wish me *mazel tov* I'm a grandmother! Sigali had a baby girl!'" She stood behind Ruthie, resting her hands on her shoulders, grateful for the change of topic but ready to propel the little girl out of the house if she resumed her questioning.

"And Moshe and Aaron and Farida and I piled in the neighbors' brand new Subaru and drove to the hospital," said Dora. She seemed to be looking beyond Farida. "We stared through the nursery window at you, Ruthie you were so tiny. Barely weighed five pounds. We couldn't understand how such a small creature could make so much noise." She smiled, but Farida saw the sorrow in her eyes.

"You have always been a wonderful friend," said Farida. And then she and Ruthie took their leave.

Chapter Twenty-Seven: Violet

Thursday, March 26, 1987

I loved our life on the kibbutz, and I remember this period as one of the happiest of my life. Of course I missed my family, the members of which were scattered throughout the country, and I missed *Ima* and Eddie who were still in Iraq. Still, I enjoyed the freedom. I worked in the dining room, which was the epicenter of our world. My sister Farida was assigned to the baby house, where she took care of the infants. The hours suited me perfectly: I was, and always have been, a morning person. Just this morning, in fact, I woke at dawn, while the rest of you slept like babies. The chirping of the birds announced the arrival of a new day. I made myself a cup of coffee and sat down, savoring each sip. This is my favorite time of day. I've always loved it, even when I was a young girl.

In the kibbutz, I would go to the dining room at four a.m. to start getting ready for the new day. The first to come were the stable workers, preparing for the morning milking. Then came the drivers, who were responsible for transporting our dairy products to Tenuvah, the country's main dairy, and for bringing fresh food from the factory back to our kibbutz. Every morning, I dragged the carts from the kitchen to the dining room, loaded them with a variety of cheeses, chopped vegetables, tuna, and fresh bread. (We ate well in the kibbutz and hardly ever felt the austerity that gripped the rest of the country.) Next, I would put up a gigantic urn of hot coffee. After that, I stacked clean dishes by the dining room door and waited for everyone to arrive.

Once the stable workers and drivers were on their way, it was the farmers men's turn. They would drink their first coffee of the morning, then go to their jobs. Finally, the children and all the other members took their turn, and the dining room would fill with jovial chaos. And I would feel utterly at home. Every so often I'd refill a platter or wipe down a table, but mostly I socialized with everyone else.

It was among the drivers that I met my first love. He was a little older than me, and his eyes were the color of the sky. He thought I was the love of his life, and he promised me the moon. The first time I saw him, my legs trembled, and the platter I was holding fell and shattered. Not what I would call an auspicious sign. He looked at me, slightly puzzled, and burst out laughing, showing his white teeth. I was so self-conscious that when I bent to pick up the fragments of the first plate, a second plate fell out of my hands and broke. In the beginning, he had no idea I had such a crush on him. Every morning I waited for him in the dining room; he would blow in like a hurricane, grab a couple of snacks, say hello, flash his brilliant smile, and disappear.

My whole life revolved around him. When I wasn't waiting for him between meals, I daydreamed about him. I'd memorized his schedule, and I tried to intercept him during the day. I knew where his room was, and I would enlist Farida to join me on night walks through the kibbutz on the off chance he'd see me from his window or we'd run into him on the road. My guess is that he sensed I was lurking, waiting to ambush him, but he never said a word. I didn't mention it, either, even after we became a couple. It was unseemly for me, an Iraqi girl from a good home, to chase after a young man. Especially an Ashkenazi Jew from Europe.

His name was Chanan, a name I found thrillingly Israeli. I'd whisper his name to myself, emphasizing the throaty *chet* sound, smiling foolishly. Chanan, Chanan, Chanan . . . Finally, one morning, he invited me to sit with him at breakfast.

"Good morning, Sigalit," he said. I was so excited all I could do was grin at him, like an idiot. I was shocked that he knew my name. I tried to respond, but I couldn't utter a single word.

His eyes shone, and he smiled his handsome, sparkling smile. My knees shook. With some difficulty, I managed to hide my trembling hands in my apron pockets. I averted my eyes, afraid they would betray my emotions, and tried again. "Good morning to you, too."

He invited me to sit and have a cup of coffee. I looked around the room, searching for the dining room supervisor. She smiled at me and nodded her consent.

For many months, Chanan was like a brother and a friend to me, sometimes a father, and, above all, a teacher. He taught me Hebrew with tremendous patience. In the beginning, we didn't talk much; my

language was still quite limited. We would walk through
the kibbutz, gazing at one another in mutual admiration.
This was enough for us. In his small room, Chanan
taught me to read and write. He sat next to me for
hours, uncovering the mysteries of the language. "Repeat
after me: *Ha-doar ba hayom / b'oto ha'adom.*" Each day
without fail I wait for the mail. It was through children's
rhymes like this one that I learned to speak Hebrew.
Chanan was Romanian by birth, and I picked up his
accent along with his vocabulary. Even today, I speak
Hebrew with a trace of both Iraqi and Romanian accents,
a confusing combination nobody can identify.

Besides Hebrew, Chanan also taught me to love the
land with my feet. On Shabbat, we went for long hikes
around the kibbutz. Occasionally we took his truck and
went farther afield. I memorized the names of rocks and
mountains; I knew the names of stones before I knew
how to construct complete sentences. "Chalkstone. Say
it: chalkstone." And with my Iraqi-Romanian accent, I
would try to repeat his words.

"Chakestone?"

"No, chalkstone," he'd say. Try it again. Chalkstone."

Because of my love for Chanan and his love for
rocks, I went on to study geology many years later.

I will never forget what Chanan did for me. For a
long time, he was my whole world. Of course, Farida was
there, too, and her presence took the edge off my
longings for my far-flung family. But for the most part, I
sought out Chanan. I tried to spend every free minute
with him.

When Dan and I got married, we invited him and his wife to the wedding. I knew they had a daughter, and that they traveled all over the world. Chanan was very curious, and loved to go on long trips. Tragically, he was killed in the Six-Day War, in one of the battles for Jerusalem.

I met Chanan's only daughter two years ago, at the university, and the resemblance between them was uncanny. When I first looked at her, I saw the contours of his beautiful face reflected in hers. Like her father, she had deep blue eyes and a glimmering smile. They had the same last name. When I asked her if she was related to the Chanan who had died in the war so many years ago, she told me she was his daughter. For a minute, I remember, I had trouble breathing, and my heart raced. Memories of our courtship washed over me like waves. I told her who I was and invited her over.

When Chanan's daughter came to the house, she asked a lot of questions, trying to reconstruct her father through my stories. She was only three years old when he died, and most of what she knew about him, she told me, came from photographs she'd seen and stories she'd heard. I understood that she was searching for her identity, and so I tried to impart as many details as possible. I told her about his hearty laugh, his good heart, his intelligence and meticulousness. Mostly I spoke of his insatiable curiosity and love for the land. She devoured every morsel of information.

But back to the kibbutz I don't want to confuse you too much. My life was good on the kibbutz from the very beginning, as I already told you. But for Farida, the change was drastic and difficult. She was a pampered child, whose life had been tidy and safe, and here she was, thrust into a harsh and callous reality. Back in Iraq, Farida had spent all her time in school or playing with friends. Our mother and father had taken care of all her needs. But here, she had to become an adult. She spoke a different language, her parents were far away, and the only person she could depend upon was me. It wasn't always easy. It's true, I was a little older than her, but don't forget that I was still young myself.

Farida loved the little babies, and after two months on the kibbutz, her Hebrew improved tremendously. She befriended the other Iraqi immigrants and gradually became less bitter. But all this would soon change. Once again, our lives were about to capsize. *Ima* and Eddie arrived from Iraq, and *Ima* decided it was time to fortify our tribe and reunite the family. She couldn't begin to imagine the hardships we were about to face. First, though, I must tell you about Eddie's and *Ima's* immigration to Israel.

Chapter Twenty-Eight: Noa

Noa finished reading of her mother's life on the kibbutz and smiled to herself. It was strange to think of her mother as a young woman, as someone who had been in love before she met Noa's father. It was stranger still to imagine Violet pursuing a young man. She had never shared this experience with her daughter, and Noa wondered why. Perhaps it was too embarrassing; or maybe she thought Noa wouldn't want to know. When Noa broke up with her high school boyfriend, she had gone crying to Violet. Her mother had been supportive, but she hadn't told her about her own unrequited love. Why had she kept this part of her life a secret? Noa couldn't explain it, and she felt disappointed, even insulted. Her mother had zealously guarded her privacy. Maybe she simply didn't want Noa intruding upon her personal love story. And yet, through her diary, she was inviting Noa in. Why had she kept so much of her life a secret? She was close to Noa but at the same time removed. She had protected, nurtured, cared for her daughter, but she had kept her heartaches to herself. Why?

Noa put down the diary. Something else occurred to her: when this story took place, her mother was younger than she herself was now, but she had shown such wisdom, such independence! It couldn't have been easy for her, being all alone, far from her family, with only a limited knowledge of the language. And the dramatic change in lifestyle, from her coddled life in Iraq to her life on the kibbutz, couldn't have been easy, either. Noa knew what kibbutz life was like; she had done her army service on a kibbutz, and the transition from her childhood home to the long hours and harsh conditions of the kibbutz had been hard for her, too. Now more than ever, Noa recognized her mother's vitality and optimism. She had learned so much about Violet in the last few weeks, and she wanted to learn more.

The following morning, Noa awoke to the dry desert winds blowing wildly. The air was thick with dust. She opened her bedroom window, then slammed it shut. Everything outside looked murky and tinted orange. Noa lay back down. In weather like this, she thought to herself, people didn't even want to stick their noses outside. Anyway, she didn't have much planned for the day. She had to make some progress with her seminar paper on Yona Wallach, that was all. Before she got started, though, she would see if Ofir was back.

She jumped up and went to the bathroom, sat on the toilet, and yawned. She brushed her teeth languidly, looking at herself in the mirror. She liked what she saw. She strolled through the apartment, naked, and went into Ofir's room. He lay on his side, one leg entangled in the blanket, the other exposed, lying hairy and muscular, dark against the white sheet. His hands were tucked beneath his head like a pillow, and he slept soundly. The sight of his innocent face aroused Noa. She wanted to caress it, this face that was at once strange and familiar, but for the next few minutes she stayed where she was.

He looks so sweet, she thought. *He looks delicious.* She walked to his bed and climbed under the covers, pressing her breasts against his back. When she nibbled on his ear and put her hand between his legs, he pushed back against her.

"Noa," Ofir whispered. "What are you doing? Don't you want me to sleep?" His voice was torpid, indulgent.

"Do you always talk in your sleep?" she said.

"Always. It's been a hobby of mine for a long time. Now come here," he whispered, turning to face her. He pulled her close and kissed her full lips, then gently licked her ear. Noa settled into his embrace, felt his racing heart, measuring her body against his, matching the movements of his body. She was overcome with desire. She didn't think about tomorrow or the next day but submitted completely to her passion. She knew he was hers, he wouldn't turn her down, she wanted his body, and she gave in to her own pleasure. She'd leave the thinking for later. Now it was time for love.

Chapter Twenty-Nine: Farida

Night descended upon the village. Inside her cramped apartment, Farida felt as if she could get lost inside her own walls. The emptiness was its own sound, rattling in her ears, filling her head with desperation. She heard everything: one couple argued, someone showered, another person flushed a toilet. In the apartment below, she heard clotheslines squeaking. These were the difficult hours. Sigal had come to take Ruthi home and left her alone. It was too late to call anyone, too late for a walk. She writhed in her bed, laying first on one side, then the other.

Giving up on the idea of sleep, Farida turned on the television and watched the late-night news. The same horrifying headlines repeated over and over: more deaths, more casualties. Fatah claimed responsibility. "Murder in the family!" announced the anchorman, and Farida had heard enough. It's not as if the news helped her sleep, she thought, and besides, there was nothing she could do. If only she could sleep like a rock at the bottom of a river, and wake refreshed the next morning after a dreamless slumber.

"Ach," she sighed, "Ach." There was nothing else she could do. She couldn't even read Violet's diary; Noa had it now. *I really must talk to that girl. I'll call her first thing in the morning,* she promised herself.

She plodded to the kitchen, reached for the pack of cigarettes on the counter. She stuck a cigarette in her mouth and burrowed through her small matchbox. She pulled out one dead match after another. "Everything is burnt out," she muttered. She removed the cover of the box and searched again for a match just one with a red tip. When she still came up empty, she threw the box into the sink and opened a drawer in the cabinet, looking for a new box. Once again, she was disappointed.

She opened every door of every cabinet and rummaged through every drawer. Nothing. She went to the bedroom and ransacked every drawer in the bureau, scattering clothes around the room. She looked on every surface, on every shelf. She even crouched painfully to search beneath the bed. Eventually she stomped to the armchair on the porch and fell into it, defeated. A black night awaited her, she thought, blacker than black. In her despair, terrible thoughts rushed into her mind: I'm abandoned here, alone; nobody needs me anymore; and I don't even have a single goddamn match!

This loneliness . . . Two years had passed since Moshe had left her a widow. She kept active during the day, but her nights were long and barren. In the last years of his life, especially when he was sick, Moshe had filled her life. Taking care of him, accompanying him to the hospital, cooking, doing laundry, constantly trying to lift his spirits all of this had kept her busy. She still hadn't adjusted to life without him. Her life seemed a deep and terrible chasm, impossible to fill. She cooked, cleaned, lent a hand to Sigal, entertained friends, but the nights . . . they were endless.

Every evening, Farida girded herself for another war against sleeplessness. When the day came to an end, and silence blanketed the neighborhood, she faced a battle she knew was lost before it even began. She prayed for the elixir of sleep and was rewarded with despair. Memories sneaked in, poked through every crack, paralyzing thoughts that tormented her. Finally, early in the morning, her harrowed, exhausted body would surrender. She usually fell asleep in the armchair. Then her daughter's daily "good morning" phone call would wake her. After several ragged nights, she would be rewarded with a one night of deep, blessed sleep. Then she'd face the cycle all over again.

The sudden ringing of the telephone shattered the silence of the night, and her heart began to race. *What had happened now? Who died?* She rushed to the phone.

"Hello, hello, who is this? What happened? Sigali?" The words tumbled out of her mouth.

"Hello, Chana?"

It was a man's voice, with the same thick Iraqi accent she had, but she didn't recognize it. "No, this isn't Chana. Chana who?"

"Hello, Chana?" It was as if he hadn't heard her.

"No," she repeated, "this isn't Chana. There's no Chana. I'm afraid you have the wrong number."

"Oh, pardon me . . . I'm so sorry . . . I hope I didn't wake you."

"I wish you had woke me up! It would have meant I was asleep."

"Oh. I was looking for Chana," the man said. "But it's okay." After a moment, he spoke in Arabic: "*Anti man Iraq?*" Are you from Iraq?

"Yes," she said in Hebrew, then switched to Arabic: "*Mi inat?*" Who are you?

"*Ana kaman man Iraq,*" said the unfamiliar voice. He was also from Iraq.

Farida smiled. She wasn't the only one in the world still awake at this late hour. And he, too, was Iraqi. She decided to learn more about this man who was also awake after the midnight broadcast of "The Daily Verse," when the only sound emanating from the television was the monotonous, miserable hiss of static. Somehow, it was understood that they would converse in Arabic, and so they did.

"What city are you from?" Farida asked.

"I'm from Basra. And you?"

"Baghdad," Farida said. "But my grandmother lived in Basra for many years, and my family lived there for awhile, too."

"Who was your grandmother? Maybe I knew her. You know how it is in Iraq," continued the anonymous voice. "Everyone knew everyone else." He sounded apologetic, hoping his candid question hadn't put her off.

"Yes." Farida smiled. "Her name was Daisy Twaina, *allah yirchama.* She was a very special woman. She went from door to door selling cloth, and she made dresses, too, and suits for the boys. She made everything," Farida said with pride in her voice. "My grandmother was widowed at a young age, and she had to make a living. I don't know if you knew her. She died when my father was just a child."

At the other end of the wire, the man patiently waited for his turn. When she was done, he said, "Give me a minute to get my brain going. I think I know who she is . . . Twaina—*Um Daoud?*' The mother of David?

"Yes, that was my grandmother! *Ya'allah*, what a memory you have! What a small world. How did you know who I was talking about? How do you know her? You must know my father, too."

"I know your grandmother because my mother used to buy her wares, and I even remember your father," he said. "Your grandmother and your father used to come to our house to sell cloth. I was only six or seven years old, but I remember them. Your father was already a young man he might have even been married. He must have been about twenty-five. He helped her he was a good son to his mother. And she . . . well, she was something else!" he gushed. "She was what we now call a feminist. She wasn't afraid of robbers she would walk around at night, during the day, in the heat, in the cold. Nothing stopped her."

Farida did some quick calculations in her head. The man she was talking to was about eight years older than her. A feeling of warmth the warmth of home filled her heart. She suddenly felt as if the walls of her house were breathing, that the suffocation she'd experienced just a few minutes earlier was abating.

"What is your name, sir?" she asked.

"I am Victor Cohen. A pleasure to meet you."

"Nice to meet you, too. My goodness, what a small world," she said. "You know, my father studied accounting during the day, then in the evening he would lug his mother's wares all over town. Even after he had a family of his own, he continued to help her, right up until my parents moved to Baghdad because of his work. You know what it meant to be an accountant in Iraq? Working for the government, no less? I can't remember him ever wearing anything besides a white suit not until he came to Israel. He helped his mother all his life, as much as he could, *Allah yirchama.*"

"Yes, good for him," Victor said. After an uncomfortable silence, he spoke again. "Okay. Well, I didn't mean to bother you. You have to sleep, don't you?"

"Sleep?" she scoffed. "What sleep? *Walla,* you're not bothering me I can't sleep. But maybe you have to sleep?" She paused, "or something. You must be a busy man: maybe you have to get up early? Or find Chana."

"No, I'm not rushing off anywhere. I've been retired for quite awhile. I'm not going to sleep, and I don't have to wake up early. In fact," he admitted, "I'm having a good time talking to you. The truth is," he said, chuckling, "I sleep very little, hardly at all. Chana is my daughter-in-law. I wanted to remind her that she's taking me somewhere tomorrow. She and my son go to sleep very late, and I just wanted to make sure she didn't forget. She's a good daughter-in-law: she comes from Haifa to Ramat Gan twice a week to bring me food and takes me to the doctor. Sometimes we even go on trips."

"So perhaps you should hang up and call her now?" Farida tried to be polite.

"No, no, it's okay," he reassured her. "I'll call her in the morning. So what happened to your family? Where do you live now?"

"I live in the southern section of Zichron Ya'akov, in an apartment complex. You know where that is?"

"No, not for the life of Allah," he laughed. "When I think of Zichron, I think of private houses."

"Oh, no! It's not only houses there are apartments dating from the fifties. I've lived here since I married my husband, Moshe, *allah yirchama*. And you're from Ramat Gan, you said?"

"From Ramat Baghdad," he joked. "That's what they call Ramat Gan, right?"

"Yes. Why did all the Iraqis decide to settle in Ramat Gan?" She liked his sense of humor.

"And you tell me, how did that bastard Saddam Hussein manage to attack our neighborhood, sending missiles straight into the houses of the same Iraqis who ran away from his country?"

Farida laughed and coughed, coughed and laughed. "You know, you're right. How come I never thought of that? Maybe that's his revenge. Bastard, may his memory be wiped out," she spit, "may his name be cursed."

On the other side of the line, Farida heard the same combination of laughter and coughing.

"Listen," he said. "I've really enjoyed talking to you. You're a lovely lady. Maybe one day I'll dial the wrong number again?"

"Maybe. Only God knows. Have a good night."

"Wait!" Victor said. "You never told me your name."

"I'm Farida. Farida Sasson."

"Nice to meet you, Farida."

After saying goodbye and hanging up, she continued to stare at the phone. *He really was a nice man,* she thought. *I hope he dials the wrong number many more times.* Their conversation had eased her loneliness. She went to her bedroom, forgetting about her customary bedtime cigarette, collapsed into her bed, and immediately fell asleep.

Chapter Thirty: Violet

Friday, April 3, 1987

Today is my birthday. At my age, I have to think hard to make sure I get my age right: I was born in 1932, which means that I have now lived through fifty-five springs. Indeed, today is a warm and pleasant spring day; even nature seems to be sharing in my celebration. From my bedroom window I can see our flower garden: primroses, anemones, narcissus, an almond tree, all dressed for the holidays, everything in bloom. I stretch my arms, and for a moment my heart fills with joy.

Yesterday, Noa called to wish me a happy birthday. And Guyush, my baby, stopped in my bedroom before leaving for school. His long, muscular body crouched down next to mine, and he pressed his warm cheek against mine. He's begun to grow some stubble, and I think he'll have to start shaving soon.

He perched at the edge of my bed and kissed my hollow cheek. My face has grown so thin, sometimes I feel like my two cheeks are collapsing into each other and becoming one. Guy wrapped his long arm around my neck and presented me with a gift wrapped in colorful paper. I thanked him and asked his permission to open it. Guy smiled. "Of course, of course, open it!" he said. Then he said, hesitantly, that he hoped I liked it.

I opened the package and found a small wooden jewelry box, painted and decorated by my sweet and talented son. The pictures he painted reflect the things I love the most. On the cover, he painted a beach, and on the bottom, two primroses, an anemone, and two tulips, all tied together. The sides of the box are painted with the colors of the sky. Tears filled my eyes, and my hands began to tremble.

"Thank you," I whispered. "Thank you so much. It's amazing. I couldn't have asked for a nicer gift."

"*Ima*, you still haven't seen what's inside," Guy said with a smile, gesturing for me to open the box.

Very carefully, I lifted the lid. Inside I found a silver pendant with the letters "Chet" and "Yud" engraved upon it: "*Chai*" life. I was speechless. The tears welling in my eyes streamed down my cheeks. I was both grateful and afraid. Who could tell what the next day would bring? Would I be here to celebrate my fifty-sixth birthday with my beloved family? Maybe not . . . and if I wasn't going to be here, who would accompany my son to the draft office? Who would wash his uniform? Cook his favorite foods? Listen to his stories? Who would support Noa when she returned to civilian life? Who would stand by her when she fell in love? Who would walk her down the aisle? Stand at her side when her first child was born? Who would share her own experiences, her own life lessons, with Noa? How could it be anyone other than me? What a cruel world, I wanted to scream, what a terrible world. I want to live!

My son hugged my bony body and stroked my back. "*Ima*, what happened? What happened to you?" he asked over and over. I saw the guilt in his eyes. I had no control over my crying; I certainly hadn't intended to cause my beloved son any pain. Just then, Dan-Dan walked in, carrying a tray laden with a lavish breakfast and two roses—one red, one white—in a vase.

My tears turned to sobs, and my sobs to hysteria. Dan-Dan understood what was going on. He looked at the jewelry box, then at the pendant clutched in my hand. Wordlessly, he joined our embrace. My two men, the loves of my life, hugged me fiercely, holding each other as well. We cried together for a long time, sitting on the bed, holding each other with such ferocity, as if our family would fall apart if we let go. If we stayed in this embrace, we would give each other the strength to go on. To live! I so want to live!

I felt like they could read my mind, like they knew exactly what was going through my head and my heart. They, too, had no idea what each day would bring. It was a very powerful experience, one I know we will all carry in our hearts for the rest of our lives. Guy was late to school, Dan-Dan was late to work, and after I sent them both on their way, I went to my study and sat down to write.

There is a lot of work ahead of me, and I have an important job to do. Whoever has no past has no future future, that's what I believe. My children, my beloved, be proud of who you are. You are the offspring of a marvelous family, you are the future. Understanding your past will give you everything you need to face your future. That is my job: to fill in the gaps in our family history, to tell you as much as I can about our family. When something is written down, it lives on forever, and even if I am not here, what I write will always be with you.

Chapter Thirty-One: Noa

Noa read and re-read the passage about the moment of healing that the three of them had shared. *Aba, Ima,* and Guy. And where was she? And why hadn't she heard about this earth-shattering experience? A sense of disappointment, tinged with envy, pulsed in her heart, and she wept. She couldn't remember if she had given her mother a gift on the last birthday of her life. All she remembered was calling her, hastily wishing her a happy birthday before running off to guard duty.

She read the words again, trying to parse the lesson her mother was trying to teach her. Was it that knowing about the past gives you the skills you need to navigate the future? Was her past the answer to the future? Did she agree with her mother's words? What skills did she now have that she hadn't had before? The image of her mother sitting in her study, leaning over her notebooks was so real, Noa felt that if she could just reach out and touch that fragile body, then Violet would turn toward her, and smile her reassuring smile.

As she delved deeper into the diary, Noa felt closer to her mother than she ever had. She believed she knew her better, understood her. There were moments when she imagined being drawn back into her mother's womb, and at those moments she felt a deep desire to be a fetus once again, nurtured and protected, whose only job was to grow. At other times, it seemed like she wasn't reading the diary but writing it that she and her mother had fused into one entity and would never be separated again.

Chapter Thirty-Two: Violet

Sunday, April 5, 1987

The excitement of my birthday has died down. Noa won't be coming home this weekend; tomorrow we will visit her. I'm glad she took my advice and stayed at the base, despite my illness. It lightens my burden to know she's happy, that she doesn't have to watch me suffer. The bond between me and Noa is unbreakable, and I know that my illness is causing her great pain. That's why it's so important to me that she lives her own life, rather than living in the shadow of my sickness. Guy is different: it seems to me that even though he is so much younger than her, he knows how to accept what cannot be changed. Noa is more sensitive, rebellious, and stubborn she tilts at windmills.

My dear children. May your journey through life take you through beautiful and beloved landscapes.

Today I will return to Iraq, to the summer of 1951. I will tell you the story of *Ima* and Eddie's grueling *Aliyah* to Israel. *Aba* was learning Hebrew in the *ulpan*, and the rest of my family was scattered among different kibbutzim. Our connection to our family in Iraq was fragile. You have to remember that we didn't have telephones back then, not in Iraq and not here. Our letters traveled circuitous paths, and sometimes it took weeks for them to arrive.

I told you how *Ima* received the *Aliyah* permits when she gave up her and Eddie's Iraqi citizenship and how she'd done it behind his back. She was waiting for the right time to broach the subject. Eddie was fearless, and, until his dying day, stubborn as an ox. I told you how he had taken it upon himself to play an active role in the underground, how he never even considered abandoning his comrades and moving to Israel. But one warm summer evening, he heard the terrible news that two of his friends from the Resistance had been captured and were being held by the authorities.

This painful news left the members of the underground in shock. There was no doubt that their captured comrades wouldn't be able to withstand the harsh interrogations and torture. They also knew that their fate was sealed: they would be hanged in the city square, a warning to everyone else. The sight of a rowdy crowd watching the execution of an alleged traitor was the hottest show in town. There was only one option: the remaining members of the Resistance had to leave immediately. Every extra minute on Iraqi soil increased their chances of death. Most members of the Resistance did not have *Aliyah* permits.

As I already told you, the primary goal of the Iraqi Resistance was to protect the Jews of Baghdad after the 1941 pogrom. When the state of Israel was declared, the Jewish plight only worsened. As their families moved to Israel, brave and talented young people volunteered to stay behind and protect the remaining Iraqi Jews. Lately, though, the Resistance fighters had come to recognize that the Iraqi Jewish community was very small: before long, they themselves would move to Israel. Now, in light of the arrest of their two comrades, they realized that the Resistance was over, and its members had to leave as soon as possible. They knew there was nothing they could do to help the two captured men.

Eddie was under a lot of pressure. Not only were the authorities about to hang two of his friends, but it wouldn't be long before they came knocking on his own door. He was besieged by guilt: why had he allowed his grandmother to stay with him? Surely she, too, would be hanged. What would happen to his mother? What about his brothers and sisters, his uncles and aunts? And what about his beloved Farida? Would he ever see her again? He wasn't so concerned with his own life, but the fate of his grandmother and the rest of the family weighed upon his heart like a stone.

Eddie hurried home to deliver the dismal news. My mother, his grandmother took his hands and quietly led him to her bedroom. She opened the closet, pulled out their *Aliyah* permits, placed them in his hands, and gazed at his face, waiting for his reaction. Eddie blanched; he couldn't believe his eyes. He knew that securing these permits was a long process. How had she done it so stealthily, behind his back, without asking him what he thought, what he wanted? She must have given up his citizenship as well! Eddie knew this had required her to forge his signature. When had she done this? And how had she hidden it from him?

After several minutes that felt like an eternity *Ima* began to speak very softly. "Now we're going to pack. We have to get out of here as quickly as we can, do you understand?" Eddie, stunned, didn't know whether to be angry or grateful. On the one hand, she had saved both their lives, but, on the other, she had forged his signature and acted against his wishes. Eddie looked in his grandmother's eyes and said nothing.

"*Ya'allah,* Eddie," she urged him. "*Ya'allah.* This is too much for us and for our family. No more games, Eddie, not unless we want our lives to end today. Any minute they'll come knocking at our door, and they'll take us straight to the town square and hang us. There's not a moment to waste, Eddie, so don't even think of arguing with me." Eddie didn't argue, he did as she said. He knew she was right, and that if he jeopardized his own life, he was jeopardizing hers as well.

They packed a small suitcase, *Ima* took what little money they had, and they left the rest behind. They stole from their house in the middle of the night and made their way to the person in charge of smuggling Jews out of Iraq. The next plane to Israel was leaving the following morning. If they made it, their lives would be saved if not . . . their fate was sealed.

Chapter Thirty-Three: Noa

As usual, Farida welcomed Noa with hugs, kisses, and a table full of treats.

"*Tfu, a hamsa on* you, you look so beautiful, a blessing on your head, your mother is so happy when she sees you from up there," she said, pointing to the ceiling.

"Come," she continued, "a blessing on your head, come have a seat. What do you want to eat? I have squash patties and bulgur patties in the freezer. You want some soup?"

"Anything is fine, Aunt Farida. You don't want me to get fat, do you?" Noa smiled. She was enjoying the attention her aunt lavished upon her.

"You mean you don't want to be fat like me?" Farida laughed, waved her hand dismissively, then continued, "Fine, fine. See, I'm watching your diet. Just have some squash patties and rice. I'm looking out for your figure, even though it wouldn't hurt you to put on a few pounds look how skinny your hands are, what, don't you eat anything?"

"Yes, of course I eat, Aunt Farida. Don't worry, my roommate makes sure I eat." Aunt Farida's transition from caretaking to ranting was beginning to grate on her nerves.

"What, a man who cooks?" Farida shrieked. "My Moshe, *Allah yirchamu,* he couldn't even make a sandwich." Farida wrinkled her nose. "So what does he make for you, this roommate?"

"All kinds of things," Noa said, defending Ofir. "He loves to cook, and he makes all kinds of food: Italian food, schnitzel, everything."

"*Nu,* so now you have to teach him to cook Iraqi food, too. Some kind of patty, maybe, or for Shabbat *tbit,* chicken with rice. What do you think?" She nudged Noa with her elbow. "He sounds very nice, this roommate. Is there something going on between you?" She shot Noa a curious look.

"Something," Noa answered, embarrassed.

"Good, good," Farida said. "I won't stick my nose in your business. If you want to tell me, you'll tell me, and if don't want to tell me, you won't. You didn't come here for an interrogation, did you?" She laughed again, coughed, and cursed the cigarettes that were shortening her life, swearing that if she weren't an old woman she would kick this disgusting habit. "But it's too late to change. It is what it is, and that's it. What do you say, Noa'le? Am I right?" She smiled at her niece.

"What do I say? I say it's never too late, Auntie, and anyway, why do you call yourself old? Look how much energy you have. I wish I had a fraction of your energy."

"*Nu,* enough already. I'm sixty years old this year, but don't you dare tell anyone. You swear?"

"Scout's honor, I won't tell anyone," Noa promised, and all of a sudden she felt terrific. It was nice being in Farida's house, looking into Farida's face. She let her aunt ramble on. Then a thought popped into her head: this little house had always been, and would always be, the one constant in her life.

She looked around and remembered scenes from her childhood. Aside from the color of the walls, the apartment was basically the same as it had always been. The kitchen cabinets had been there when she was a child. Aunt Farida and Uncle Moshe's bedroom was exactly the same. Even Sigali and Oren's bedrooms had remained untouched. The giant bookcase sat where it always had, its shelves sagging under the weight of many books. The only change was that the children's beds had been replaced by a pull-out sofa so children and grandchildren would have a place to sleep. Usually, this meant Oren, his wife, and his kids, who would come down from the northern part of the country to visit.

Noa felt a tightening in her chest. She remembered how she and Sigali used to "rest" on the giant porch every afternoon. A nap was part of the daily routine at Aunt Farida's house. Farida would say, "Between two and four, everyone in this house rests. If you want your mother or your aunt to be pleasant and cheerful, then you have to be absolutely quiet. If you choose not to be quiet, then boy, are you going to get it." In truth, Noa knew, this was an empty threat. Aunt Farida never punished anyone. She never tried to mute the joyful chaos that took over the house when the cousins got together.

The summer heat peaked during the afternoon hours. In the small apartment, the air was stale, hot, and suffocating. On the porch, though, where Farida would spread light blankets over the cool floor for the girls to rest on, you couldn't even tell that it was summertime. It seemed like a cool wind always blew above them.

It was on this porch that she first read Devorah Omer's marvelous works. *Up and High, Sara Aharonson: Heroine, My Father's Son* these were the books that had shaped her personality, had instilled within her a fierce love for her country. Here she read *White Fang,* here she devoured *The Secret Seven* series, which had inspired her and Sigali to search for adventures and spy on suspicious-looking people in their little town.

She would never forget how the two of them used to follow one of the neighbors. They chose him because he would look to both sides whenever he walked down the street. Convinced he was a Russian spy giving information to the enemy, they tailed him constantly until they discovered he was having an affair with a married woman in the next town over. Here, on this porch, the two girls embroidered their dreams, which were largely based on the fairy tales they had read. One day, they imagined, a prince would come handsome and rich as a sultan who would whisk them off to a faraway palace made of gold. They would be *lady-ot* their Hebrew version of "ladies." Noa remembered how the word "*lady-ot*" sounded when Farida said it, with her thick Iraqi accent. The two girls would have servants they would address in English. The cousins would rule the palace. "Yes, my lady. Certainly, my lady. No problem, my lady." The servants would curtsy before they left. Most of what they imagined was based on the British television series Upstairs, Downstairs.

"Hello? Where are you? I'm talking and talking, and you're not even here!" Farida's voice shook Noa out of her reverie.

"I'm sorry," Noa stammered. "I was just thinking about how this house is the most stable thing in my life . . . how nothing here has really changed." As soon as she spoke, Noa felt guilty, as if she had betrayed her mother's memory.

An awkward silence followed. Farida settled onto one of the small kitchen chairs that by some miracle didn't collapse under her weight. Perhaps the chairs had gotten used to it.

"Noa, Noa, Noa," Farida sighed, wiping a bead of sweat from her forehead. "Walls are just walls. Home is *here,*" she said, and she placed her soft warm hand on Noa's heart. "I know that's not what you think right now, but one day you'll wake in the morning and understand you've been home the whole time."

"It's hard for you," Farida continued, "with *Aba* gone, right?"

"It's hard," Noa admitted.

"I know, my dear, I know. By God, it's hard, but it will be alright, Noa." She gave her niece a wan smile, as if to say that the two of them shared the same destiny.

"And what about *Ima's* diary?" Farida asked. "Have you read it yet?"

"I'm reading it," Noa said, turning to stare out the kitchen window. "Every page is a new adventure; every page I learn something new about *Ima.*"

"Good," Farida said. "I'm glad. It's good you're reading it. When I gave you the diary, I was afraid you wouldn't have the courage to open it." Farida placed her hands on her knees. "The diary will help you 'get your head around it,' as they say." She looked at the floor for a moment, and Noa almost spoke, but instinct told her to wait. "You know, if you keep reading, maybe you'll find the home I was talking about." She was quiet again. *A rare event, this quiet*, thought Noa. Farida continued quietly: "A home is what you get from your parents, and it will always be there." She gestured toward Noa's chest. "I know it's hard for you now, with your father gone, but you have to understand that you already have everything you need to live the life you want to lead. And one day, when you have children of your own, you'll want them to feel that no matter where they go, their home will always be there, in their heart. That's what we call *roots*. And thank God, we have strong roots." Farida stared out the kitchen window. Then she turned to Noa and said, "You know what? Why don't you bring the diary here one day, so we can read it together. What do you think?"

"I promised Guy I would finish it quickly so he could read it. I'm eager to see his reaction."

"When did you say you'd give it to him?" Farida said, and Noa was surprised to hear an edge to her voice. "That wasn't my intention when I gave you the diary."

"I'll give it to him when I'm finished, and I'm hoping he'll read it quickly so the two of us can talk about it."

"Guy read quickly?" Farida said. "You're better off waiting for the *Mashiach*. You know Guy. He'll read it three times, then he'll put it out of his mind. And there's no way he'll be willing to discuss it with you."

Noa smiled sadly. "You're probably right."

"How far have you gotten?" Farida asked.

"I've read more than half. Mostly about life in Iraq . . . a little about their journey to Israel."

"Excellent," said Farida. "And how did it feel?"

"It wasn't easy at first. The truth is," said Noa, "it still isn't easy. *Ima's* presence is so real—sometimes when I read I feel like she's standing right next to me."

"Ah, that's exactly what I expected from you, my Noa." The smile returned to Farida's face. "You're the kind of person who takes chances. You took one chance after another, and you were never afraid. What is it they say? *A coward dies a thousand deaths, a hero dies but once.*" She laughed but there was no mirth in it. "You'll see," Farida continued. "It'll be okay. I've already told you, and I'll tell you again: you're very strong on the inside. The Twaina-Yishayahu women can deal with anything."

Farida stood and began wiping down counters. Then she asked if Noa was interested in hearing some family stories.

Noa never objected to hearing stories. She loved hearing her aunt's tales: about her mother, kibbutz, and the transit camp; about how Violet used to study for her exams on the very thick branches of a wild strawberry tree (it was a huge one), in her parents' garden, the only place that afforded her some measure of peace and quiet. Noa lay on the sofa, stretched her limbs, and waited for her aunt to speak.

Chapter Thirty-Four:
Violet, Winter of 1951

The next morning, after a tense and terrified night, Eddie and *Ima* boarded an airplane that took them to Cyprus, then on to Israel. We found out later that the Iraqis had a bounty on Eddie's head. His survival was truly miraculous, and so was *Ima's*. When they arrived in Israel, they were surprised to learn they would have to traverse the entire country to see the entire family. First they visited *Aba*, who had been living in the transit camp in Ramle, which is located in the canter of Israel; then they went on to a kibbutz in the north to see my sister Chabiba. Their reunion with her was extremely emotional; Chabiba hadn't seen her son in over a year. Only later did *Ima, Aba*, Chabiba, and Eddie come to the kibbutz where Farida and I lived, which is located very close Jerusalem. And even though thirty-something years have passed since that day, I still shudder with joy when I think of that meeting.

They arrived midday. Nobody had told us that *Ima* and Eddie were in Israel, so when I saw them from a distance, I figured my mind, so full of longing, was deceiving me. The cafeteria sat on a hill overlooking the main entrance to the kibbutz. While clearing tables, I saw the four of them approaching. My heart nearly stopped beating as I stood there, still as a pillar. When I recovered, I threw down my dishrag and ran to meet them. I ran like I was possessed; it was one of the longest runs of my life. It felt like it took an hour. When I finally reached them, I collapsed against *Ima's* chest, then Eddie's, and we all cried shamelessly. I immediately took them to Farida, who was working in the nursery, with those sweet little babies, and once again there were kisses, hugs, laughter, and tears.

When we calmed down, we took our honored guests to the dining room, where I introduced them to all the workers. *Ima* thanked them for taking such good care of her youngest daughter. *Ima*, who knew very little Hebrew and loved attention, enjoyed practicing the new language, and she even garnered a few compliments. After our guests had eaten and drunk their fill, swapped stories, and shared experiences, *Aba* and *Ima* informed us of their desire to reunite the family. They said they knew it was what everyone wanted, and that we two sisters would share their tent in the transit camp. The smile that had been illuminating my face disappeared instantly. I wasn't prepared for this. I really did miss my family, and I had been dreaming about the moment we would all be together, but living in the kibbutz was good for me. Living in a tent, on the other hand, didn't appeal to me at all. And how would I stay in touch with my boyfriend, Chanan?

Ima's face lit up as she described our reunion, how we would finally be reunited, with *Aba* and my older brothers (who had never taken to kibbutz life). It would be just like it used to be, she said. *Ima* had her own dreams, and she had no idea how many hardships awaited us. She promised that within a month, two at the most, we would get an apartment, which at that time seemed like a palace. In the meantime, she explained, we would live in the *ma'abara* the transit camp. "Everyone lives in the *ma'abara*. It's actually very nice," she said in her most persuasive tone. They still needed to iron out a few details, she said, but in a few weeks they would return and take us with them.

When our guests left for the *ma'abara*, Farida and I sat deep in thought. I was confused. I missed my family fiercely, but the thought of leaving Chanan was excruciating. Farida was much more pleased by *Ima's* announcement. She was always a mama's girl, and besides, she was in love with Eddie, and wherever he went was where she wanted to be. That's how it is when you're in love you can't see or hear anything else, especially when you're seventeen years old. I, on the other hand, was full of curiosity, and I was hardy. Kibbutz life suited me. But despite my mixed feelings, the thought of arguing with *Ima* never crossed my mind. How could I object to her plan? I was raised under the principle that there is nothing in the world more important than family. Family trumped everything. We were expected to obey our parents, not defy them. And I who had always been so rebellious decided I was not mature enough to resist. I had to put myself in *Ima's* hands and follow her wishes.

Chapter Thirty-Five: Farida

Later that night after Noa had returned to Tel Aviv, after cleaning the house and washing the dishes, after brewing herself a strong cup of sweet herbal tea Farida sat on the porch and looked into the gathering darkness.

The nights were hot, almost unbearable, and mosquitoes buzzed in her ears. They would disappear later, but at dusk, when the air seemed to stand perfectly still, mosquitoes descended on her, like vultures on carrion. The evening was warm and humid, and Farida was desperate to escape both the mosquitoes and the terrible heat.

She went to get the fan from the kitchen. If she adjusted it so that it blew directly into her face, not only would the mosquitoes keep their distance, but she'd also stop sweating so much. She returned with the fan, set it up, sank into her armchair, took a deep breath, and smiled triumphantly. This time she had the upper hand. She had outsmarted the mosquitoes. Let them fly somewhere else, bother someone else; it was no longer her problem. She savored the cool breeze and the beautiful silence.

The phone rang. She heaved herself out of her chair. Because of the late hour, she thought it was likely a wrong number. She didn't dare hope it might be Victor calling back.

"Hello, Farida?" It was a masculine voice, but she couldn't tell if it sounded familiar or not.

"Yes, this is Farida. Who's this?" Farida kept her tone business-like.

"Hello, it's me, Victor Cohen, the one who dialed the wrong number. Do you remember me?"

"Hello, Victor. Of course I remember you! How are you?" Farida found herself grinning.

"*Walla*, what can I say? *Ana Araf?* Do I know? This hurts, that hurts that's what it is to get old."

He seemed earnest, but Farida couldn't help being suspicious. "What happened?" she said. "Did you dial the wrong number again?"

"No, this time it wasn't a mistake. I had to call half the world to reach you. Do you know how many 'Sassons' there are in the 06 area code? Twenty, maybe, and not a single Farida Sasson."

Farida didn't know what to think. What should she say to Mr. Victor, who had searched half the world to find her? "*Walla*, good for you, Victor. Of course you couldn't find my name my number is listed under my husband Moshe's name, *Allah yirchamu.*"

"I figured it was under your husband's name, which I didn't know. But today I reached your sister-in-law, Malka, and she gave me your number."

"You reached Malka?" Farida laughed nervously. She was embarrassed, but at the same time flattered. He had tried so hard to reach her, and she hoped she knew why, but she was afraid of giving in to that hope. After weighing whether or not she could ask him such a direct question, she decided to let him get there on his own.

"That was my seventh phone call," Victor confessed. "She told me she was your sister-in-law, and she gave me your number . . . I hope I didn't wake you this time?"

"Not at all! Wake me?" she waved her hand dismissively. "I spent the day with my Noa, the daughter of my sister of blessed memory. A lovely girl, what else can I tell you. A blend of Iraqi and Ashkenazi."

"It does sound like an excellent mix," Victor said. He coughed. "You're probably wondering why I'm calling you out of the blue," he said, then coughed again and apologized. Farida tried to put him at ease.

"Victor, it's really okay. I'm glad you called." She sat in the chair next to the telephone; she felt like a girl again, like someone was courting her. It felt nice. She particularly enjoyed knowing that Victor had gone out of his way to contact her, and that, like a young man, he was having trouble explaining why he had called.

"Actually, it's important," Victor said earnestly. "After I hung up, I remembered something, and it kept me up all night. I decided I had to find you and ask you a question."

"*Tfadal*," Farida said. Please. She felt a rush of disappointment. Maybe he wasn't courting her after all.

"I wanted to tell you that I think I know you. Tell me, did your family once live in a neighborhood in Lod?"

"Yes, my parents got an apartment there after spending two-and-a-half years in a transit camp in

Ramle." She tried hard to remember who this Victor might have been, this man who said he knew her, but she came up with nothing.

"I knew it was your family!" Victor whooped. "What a small world. I knew your father when I was a boy, but by the time we got to Israel I was already a young man, and I didn't remember him anymore. Then I met this Iraqi guy who worked with me at the post office Eddie, his name was and he had just moved to Lod from Ramle. And one day he invited me for Friday night dinner. While I was there, I remember, your father told me he was the chief accountant of the Iraqi government. Do you see what I'm saying? When I hung up the phone after our conversation, I got to thinking. I did the math, and I came to the conclusion that he was the son of *Um Daoud.* Do you see? I knew Eddie's parents from Iraq!" Victor was breathless. "How many Jewish accountants worked for the Iraqi government? Suddenly I realized *walla,* Victor, this man whose house you were in, he was the son of Daisy Twaina! And you were just talking to his daughter!"

Farida could hardly believe what Victor was saying. But the details he recounted were accurate. Victor Cohen not only knew her father, but he knew her Eddie. He'd even dined with her family in Lod, it pleased her that this was so.

Victor paused to catch his breath, and then continued: "Eddie brought me to your house one day, and I was very impressed. What a warm home, what beautiful Shabbat songs . . . we even danced on the grass.

I think you had long black hairand you sang. Am I right?"

"No, not me. You must be talking about my sister Violet. I don't like to sing, but she did, and what a lovely voice she had; it was really something. No, you're talking about my sister. I was the other girl. I did have black hair, but it was only down to my shoulders. A bob, it was called. To this day I can't sing like she did. *Walla,* good for you, what a memory you have!"

"Well, do you remember me?" Victor sounded hopeful. "A tall man with green eyes?"

"Yes. No." Farida was confused. "No," she finally admitted, "I have no idea who you are."

"That's okay," Victor said. "It doesn't matter. I worked with Eddie for a month or two, then he left. I heard he was killed later on."

For a moment, neither of them spoke. "I was very sorry to hear it," Victor said.

"Yes, it was very hard for us, losing Eddie. It's still hard," she confessed. "Eddie was something else, as they say. He was special. And to die young, like he did, that really hurt." Farida wiped away a tear. It's a good thing Victor couldn't see her, she thought to herself. She was starting to like this man. He was willing to make an effort. He was curious and generous. She knew how expensive these calls were. He wasn't rushing her, wasn't counting his pennies. He was patient. What else could she ask for on a hot summer night?"

"So you see? That's why I had to find you . . ." He sounded embarrassed.

She waited a moment before speaking. "And do you remember me?"

"I'll tell you the truth," Victor began, then cleared his throat, and Farida understood this was a sign of discomfort, and she decided his shyness was kind of charming. "I don't remember you, either," Victor said. Then he laughed, and it came out in a short staccato burst. Farida joined him, and the two laughed together, about life, and about coincidence.

"Listen," Victor suggested. "Now that we know each other a little bit, maybe we can meet in person. What do you think?"

"Maybe," said Farida. It was still a little too soon for her to meet him, she thought.

Victor, as if reading her mind, said, "You know what? Can I call you again tomorrow?"

"Of course—why not?" Farida was relieved that he wasn't pushing her to meet, that he would call instead.

"Well. So now I will bid you good night, and I'll call you tomorrow. Okay?"

"Sure, no problem," Farida replied, satisfied.

"What's a good time for me to call?" he asked politely.

"Evenings are good. After eight," she said. She didn't know why she had picked eight and not seven or nine, or why had she told him to call in the evening and not the morning, but that's what had come out. She wished him pleasant dreams, then hung up. She felt she was going to faint from the heat. She hurried to the kitchen to find a cigarette and matches, took them out to the porch with her, and collapsed into her chair. The heat was oppressive, and sweat dripped down from her face and onto her dress. She turned on the fan, and it cooled the room quickly. But she knew a sleepless night awaited her.

Chapter Thirty-Six: Noa

Noa got off the bus near her house. It was late, and the streets, usually bustling, were empty. She liked to walk. Walking, especially when she was by herself, helped her organize her thoughts. Her visit to Farida's had been delightful and delicious as always, and the things she had learned were significant. Aunt Farida had been trying to tell her something important, something valuable. She'd wanted Noa to understand that home is something inside of you. At the moment, however, that was not what Noa believed. She felt that her home no longer existed, and she was struggling to come to terms with it.

The whole trip, from Zichron Yaakov to Tel Aviv, Noa had tried to memorize what her aunt had told her. Perhaps, she thought, if she repeated it to herself like a mantra, she would begin to believe it. Then maybe she'd feel better about herself. Happier. Maybe instead of feeling fractured, she would start to feel whole. Noa looked around her, searching for reassurance, and she found it. The fact that her surroundings looked utterly normal was a comfort in itself. The evening was hot and dry, the porch doors stood wide open, voices from televisions echoed in her ears, an occasional car whizzed past. When she walked by the playground, she heard the chirping of birds. On one porch someone strummed a guitar, a baby cried. An older man with a little dog strolled by, Noa smiled and wished the man a pleasant evening. He responded in kind, and Noa felt a sense of comfort and belonging. Everything was familiar; everything was as it should be. The world still spun; there hadn't been any catastrophes. Many changes had taken place in a short time in Noa's life, and sometimes she felt she felt overwhelmed by the pace. When she reached her apartment building, she unlocked her mailbox and took out the letter she found there. She recognized her father's handwriting and tore open the envelope, climbed the three flights of stairs, reading as she walked.

June 30, 1993

Dear Noa,

I arrived in Seattle ten days ago. So far, all I've managed to do is go for a few short hikes and take a one-day trip to Mount Rainier. Mostly I've slept. The time difference has wreaked havoc on my system: I'm sleepy during the day, and at night as the city goes to sleep I'm raring to go. The day I got here, the weather was ideal. I fell in love with this lush, lake-filled place before I even got off the plane. I was able to get a close-up look at Mount Rainier, which is covered in snow the entire year, and I was awed by its size. Less than two days later, though, the rain came and hijacked the summer, and it hasn't let up since. The locals joke that if you ask a seven-year-old boy when the sun will shine, he responds, "How should I know? I'm only seven!" In other words, it rains here most of the time, which is why everything is so green. Truthfully, the incredible view, and the chance of having even one beautiful day, compensates for all the rain. Seattle is dotted with lakes and surrounded by mountains. As I said, I fell in love with the city, and with its people. Everything is calm, nobody is in a hurry, civility and patience are the norm. Unbelievable, truly a different world.

It is strange, Noa, being here without you, without Guy, and especially without Ima. You know that Ima was my best friend, and that the two of us loved to travel the world together. It's hard for me to see all this beauty without having her at my side to share it with me. Whenever I see something interesting, I immediately think about what she would have said, how thrilled she would have been with these views, how impressed she would have been with the city's generosity and patience, how she would have enjoyed the wonderful farmer's market. She would have loved simply walking through the streets.

As I describe all this to you, I feel like I am talking to my closest friend, who also happens to be my daughter. What good luck! I hope that this finds you healthy and happy, and that you will come visit soon so we can travel together.

Warmest regards to Guy. I'll write to him soon.

Love,
Aba

Chapter Thirty-Seven: Violet

Tuesday, April 7, 1987

This morning I stood before the mirror in my bedroom and looked at myself. Usually I try to ignore the mirror, try to walk right by without so much as a glance. But this morning I dragged in a chair from the next room and sat and looked at myself naked. I didn't cover my body at all. Didn't wrap it in a robe (not even to avoid the morning chill). I didn't cover my hair with a wig, and I didn't put on makeup. I sat down and looked at myself as I was. I had given this a lot of thought and waited for the right moment: when the house was empty, when nobody could walk in unexpectedly. Dan was at work, Noa was in the army, and Guy was at school. I could no longer run away from myself. This is what I am, I decided, in my nakedness, my baldness, my atrophied body.

I directed my gaze to my bare feet. It was best to start there, I thought; then maybe I would get the courage to scan the entire length of my body until my eyes met their reflection, until I could be a witness to the naked truth, so to speak. My feet looked as tiny and delicate as they were twenty, thirty years ago. They looked nice not too big, not too clumsy, familiar. I paused for a minute, trying to decide if I was brave enough to lift my gaze. I decided I would do it slowly and carefully, and I gave myself a loophole: I didn't have to look at my entire body if I didn't want to. But, I thought, I did want to.

Slowly, slowly, I raised my eyes and cast a tentative glance at my knees, my thighs, my genitals. It was like a personal CT scan no hospital, just me, in my own bedroom, scrutinizing my body. I stared at the familiar spots. There was not a single hair on my legs or my sexual organs. My genitals looked virginal, as if they had never experienced a man, never experienced childbirth. My legs looked old and withered, and for a moment I debated whether or not to continue. I turned around and examined my back and buttocks. A dark birthmark stretched across my lower back, a covenant between me and my mother. My buttocks sagged; they had lost their former fullness and succulence. Still, I joked to myself, they did their job. I looked at the mirror with increasing contempt.

My belly was next. At the sight of the sagging pouches of skin resting on my abdomen, my eyes filled with tears and fury. Where is my body, once so fresh and young, so muscular and vital? "What's left of me?" I whispered. "What remains?" I didn't know how to answer. I turned from the mirror and leaned back in the chair, wrapping my arms around myself. I cried for a long time. My nose ran and my eyes dripped, but I didn't wipe the tears away. I let them stream down my face until they dried. I have to get back to my reflection, I commanded myself. I have to know exactly who I am, what I am, inside and out, from every corner and every angle. Be brave, I instructed myself, and I turned to face the mirror. This time I would scan myself in reverse: I'd start at the top and work my way down. I don't want to give in, I thought, I don't want to take pity on myself. The truth, that's what I'm after, the truth, right here, right now!

I looked directly at the mirror; my eyes met themselves. Dark irises ringed with grayish-black circles stared back at me. I looked for a long time, evaluating every wrinkle, every hue. There were no lashes above my eyes, no eyebrows on my forehead; only my two naked pupils staring at me. Eyes at once fearless and compassionate. Compassionate toward what? I wondered, and I knew the answer: toward myself. Maybe my body was tired and slack, embarrassing, offensive, maybe even treacherous, but in my eyes I saw life, light, strength, emotion, and a trace of wisdom. I smiled. Even my sunken cheeks no longer bothered me. I am here, I am alive and breathing. The body is just an envelope, an outer layer. Myself, my essence, my soul, these cannot be taken from me. Not by time or sickness or even death.

This is who I am, at times of peace and at times of war. The war for my life. Now I knew. I had to look at myself in the mirror and see the whole picture, from my feet to my head. It took courage to do this I balked, but I persisted, and I am proud of that. I had already looked at every part of my body. Now, if truth is what I was after, I had to look at my body as a whole. I stood opposite the mirror, erect and unyielding, looking not for war but for peace. I wanted to make peace with my body, with my God, with my destiny. The short woman standing across from me was flawed and weak, but she was whole both inside and out.

Chapter Thirty-Eight: Violet

Wednesday, April 8, 1987

Three weeks after they arrived in Israel, Eddie and *Ima* sent me and Farida a letter that changed the course of our lives. We had a double tent near the Ramle intersection, *Ima* wrote, at the outskirts of the city. We had neighbors on only one side. We were given this prime piece of property because of Eddie's work in the Resistance, and now that we had, thank God, a tent, now that everyone had left Iraq, it was time for the family to reunite. On the following Tuesday, with God's help, Eddie would come with one of his friends, they would load us and our meager possessions onto a truck, and take us to the Ramle intersection.

The letter was matter-of-fact, aside from the inclusion of copious religious expressions, phrases that would eventually disappear from our family's vocabulary. With the exception of *Aba*, who stayed religious until his dying day, the rest of us including *Ima* became secular. The letter did not contain a single expression of love, nor did it mention what awaited us in the future. Farida and I had only three days to get organized, say goodbye, come to terms with the idea that, once again, our lives were about to undergo a drastic change.

I spent the three days with Chanan. We roamed the hills of Jerusalem, stopped for a picnic in the afternoon, talked at length about the future, imagining what it held in store for us. The day before my departure, we went for an early morning hike so that we could take advantage of the entire day, and in the afternoon we stopped to rest on the banks of the Achziv Stream. Chanan said it wasn't so bad, my leaving the kibbutz. He promised to visit, but I told him he might as well forget about being a couple, because in my culture that wasn't acceptable. If *Ima* found out about our courtship, her heart would break. And *Aba*? He would have been furious. "What was was," I told him, as if I were the more mature one. Chanan couldn't understand these cultural mores, and he tried to convince me that here, in Israel, my parents would surely change, they would surely understand that their new home was more progressive than Iraq, that here girls could go out with boys and not marry right away. But then he grew silent and thoughtful.

I kept my thoughts which were dismal to myself. What kind of future awaited me without Chanan? I wondered. What awaited him? It would be best for him to forget about me and find himself another girlfriend. I'd be okay. I was completely unprepared for what happened next. Chanan took my hand, kissed it gently, looked straight into my eyes, and said: "What if we got married?"

His words stunned me. "What are you talking about, getting married?" I sputtered. "I'm only nineteen!" As much as I loved Chanan, I wasn't ready to think about marriage. We had just migrated to Israel. I had experienced only a small taste of freedom. My whole life was before me. How could I explain to Chanan that it wasn't even up for discussion? He released my hand; he was hurt. "If that's the case," he said, "then maybe it is a good thing you're leaving." These words cut me. My eyes filled with tears. All I wanted was to return to my room and never see Chanan again. We were silent as we walked back to the kibbutz. Chanan didn't say goodbye to me when Eddie arrived, and I didn't say goodbye to him. I left my broken heart at the kibbutz and set off for my new life.

Chapter Thirty-Nine: Noa

The life you have
is the life you lived
look back with understanding
find the point of genesis
the creation
create yourself
it's the best world
the only one
you could create
all this is found in you
discover it
begin from the beginning . . .

(Translated by Linda Stern Zisquit
Let the Words: Selected Poems of Yona Wallach)

Noa sat at her desk in her room and wrote: In her poem "The Life you Have," from the book Appearance, Yona Wallach writes about creation, renewal, disintegration, reconstruction, and ultimately acceptance. We must accept what is, she says, because this is all that we have. Before we can start anew, we must be strong, and that strength comes from stripping away the outer layers and delving into the deepest level of understanding. "Make amends," says Wallach, implying that we have no choice but to repair, to search, to reveal, to understand. This is our mission, our job, our destiny.

Noa put down her pen and took a moment to think about what she had read and what she had written so far. She thought about her discussion with Aunt Farida and about what her mother was trying to tell her. Violet had tried to stare down the truth, to experience revelation and recognition. She was trying to create herself; that was the purpose of the diary. Maybe that was what Noa herself had to do. Did she have to create herself, by herself? To start from the beginning? To make amends? She gazed out the window of her room at the dark skies. Autumn had arrived, with its sweet smell of falling leaves and dry parched earth, and she saw a few tiny raindrops hit the glass. Not the real rain of winter, but enough to make her feel that a new wind was blowing. She closed her eyes and took a deep breath. This evening she would see her old lover, Ehud. She wouldn't be seeing him alone, but she knew he'd be at the youth movement's reunion at the Yarkon Park.

She wondered if what she was feeling was excitement or fear. Anxiety gnawed at her stomach. She had asked Ofir to accompany her, but he was on duty that evening; she would have to deal with this alone. She lay in her bed, stretched out her body, spread her arms wide. She let the thoughts sneak in quietly. Maybe if she concentrated very hard, she could prepare herself for this meeting. She wouldn't let him slip away again. It was the truth she was after, and she would demand the truth from him, too. She wanted to move on, and the feeling buried deep inside her refused to recede. She looked at the clock; she had one more hour. How would she get him to speak to her? What could she say to keep him from ignoring her? She rose from the bed, moved to the bathroom to take a shower. When she returned to her room there was a note taped to her bedroom door. "I'm leaving, Noa. I didn't want to bother you. I'll be back at midnight. Wait up for me."

She looked at the familiar handwriting and smiled to herself. But then a feeling of guilt swept over her. Was there room in her heart for Ofir's love? Maybe it was time to work on her own "repairing." She was piecing together the fragments of her life; she was closing circles. Perhaps later, after she had closed all the circles, she would have the strength to start a new one.

Noa grabbed a pair of jeans draped over the chair and put them on. She pulled a shirt from the open closet and slipped into it. She donned a denim jacket and looked at herself in the mirror. She didn't want Ehud to pay attention to her because of her appearance. She wanted to go beyond the surface. She slammed the door behind her and headed down the steps to the street.

Chapter Forty: Farida

Friday was a very slow day; the hands of the clock refused to budge. Farida had cooked for Shabbat; she had cleaned the house; and now time stood still. Oren had told her at the last possible minute that he and his family couldn't make it: his son had come down with chicken pox. This weekend, there would be no guests for Shabbat dinner. Sigali's children were with their father, and Sigali wanted to rest.

Dora had been over that morning, taking a little break from her husband. He was driving her crazy, sitting in front of the TV all day and not saying a word. If only he were working, she complained, and then at least she could talk to the walls. When he was home, she had confided to her dear friend, she was too embarrassed to talk to the walls. The two of them sat together for a long time, drinking Turkish coffee, talking about the past, and their families, and their neighbor, Carmella, who'd had a heart attack a few days ago, when she was home alone. She'd barely managed to crawl to the phone and call an ambulance. She was at Hillel Yaffe Hospital. Everyone was there with her: all her children, and her sisters, who had hardly spoken to her for the last five years, but now apparently remembered they had a sister. They were all gathered around her bed, waiting on her. All those years she was alone, and nobody cared because she never complained. Everything was always okay; she was always smiling, even though her children almost never came to visit, and she visited them even less. And suddenly they remembered her. "Maybe they're worried about their inheritance," Dora suggested. Whatever the case, Carmella was in the hospital, sighing and groaning and letting her relatives tend to her, even though she'd admitted to Farida and Dora that she felt fine. She just didn't want to go back to an empty house.

In the afternoon, Farida tried to take a nap, but she writhed sleepless in her bed. She got up and turned on the TV. Every now and then she would venture out on the porch to check on the outside world. In her neighborhood, Fridays were special. You could see all the families walking to synagogue; hear the clanking of the pots from the kitchens. You could even hear people singing *zemirot*. There were almost no cars on the road. The hands of the clock weren't moving.

When she'd told Victor to call at eight, she never imagined she'd sit and wait for the phone to ring. Why was she feeling like this? She didn't even know what he looked like. Not only that, she knew almost nothing about him. And would she even want to know about him? When it was almost eight o'clock, she began pacing around the phone impatiently. And then, at eight precisely, the phone rang. She pounced on it and plopped down in her armchair. When she heard the familiar voice, she breathed a sigh of relief. Her sigh was so loud, so nasal, that Victor wasn't certain he'd dialed the right number.

"It's me, Farida! Of course it's me," she reassured him. "How are you, Victor?" She tried to mask her excitement.

"Great, great, everything's great." He didn't elaborate.

Desperate to fill the silence, Farida told him that her children weren't coming for Shabbat dinner because her little nephew was sick. So she had all this food. Victor told her that his twin grandsons were spending Shabbat on the army base, that they were both in combat units. "May God protect them," Farida said. Then she tried to steer the conversation to what interested her the most: Victor himself.

"I have one son and three grandchildren: a twenty-three-year-old girl and nineteen-year-old twins," Victor told her. "When I moved to Israel, I met my wife at the transit camp in B'nei Brak. We got married, and we were lucky: my business did very well. Little by little, we built a good life for ourselves. We bought a house in an old neighborhood in Ramat Gan, and we lived there for thirty-eight years. She was a good woman, my wife, and one day, when I wasn't home, she had a stroke. She deteriorated quickly and died two months later. All my life, she had taken care of me, and in the end she wouldn't even let me take care of her." Victor stopped speaking. Farida suspected he was on the verge of tears.

"Good for you," Farida said. "You're a good man. Show me another husband who wants to take care of his wife. Really, I admire you."

"You took care of your husband, right?"

"Yes, of course I took care of him, but there's a difference between a wife looking after her husband and a husband looking after his wife. Maybe my views are outdated, but that's how it seems to me. But you, you should be proud of yourself. You're a good man," she repeated. She could feel her heart beating and the sweat emanating from her body. This man impressed her more and more.

"*Walla*, what can I tell you?" said Victor. "That's life—you never know what's coming. But if you don't mind telling me," he said, "what was it like for you, living here in Israel?"

"Oh!" Farida was caught off guard. "You want to know about my life? It was life, that's all. Things didn't turn out the way I thought they would. I was in love with Eddie, the Eddie that you knew."

"Eddie?" Victor was surprised. "But wasn't he your sister's son?"

"He was my sister's son, but he was quite a bit older than me," she answered, trying to justify herself. She smiled to herself and lit a cigarette, preparing for a long conversation. "I think I loved him for as long as I could remember, and I dreamed of marrying him. It never even crossed my mind that we wouldn't get married. I had my heart set on him. Him alone."

"May his soul rest in peace," Victor said, and for a moment neither of them spoke. Then Victor asked quietly, "How did Eddie die? I swear on the Torah, Farida, I don't want to upset you, but if it's not too hard for you to talk about . . . I would really like to know what happened."

"It's alright, Victor," Farida said sadly. "Many years have passed since then. For a long time, I couldn't even speak his name, because my heart ached so much, and even now, my heart still weeps for him. But at least I can say his name, and I can even tell you what happened."

"Are you sure?" asked Victor. She wondered if he regretted asking the question.

Farida sighed. She extinguished her first cigarette, lit another, and began her story. "In Iraq, Eddie was a member of the Resistance, and we stockpiled ammunition in our house. In a storage area we used to call a *slick*. We all lived together, you know, along with other members that the Iraqis, may their name be cursed, were searching for. Once a Kurdish boy came to us, one of the people the Iraqis were after. We were trying to smuggle him into Israel. He lived with us for a month before the Resistance finally got him out of the country."

"I knew Eddie was in the Resistance," Victor said, "but I didn't know there was a *slick* in your house. Or that you hid people."

"We hid people; we hid arms; we did everything that had to be done," Farida said. She thought about how many children there were in the house, and how her parents and her older brothers had agreed to help the underground movement, even though they knew that if the Iraqis ever found out, they would murder everyone in the house, children as well as adults.

"Good for you, really, good for all of you," Victor murmured.

"When we got to Israel," Farida continued, "we lived in a transit camp in Ramle for almost two years. What can I tell you? It wasn't much of a life. There were snakes in the summer and floods in the winter; the summers were sweltering and the winters were freezing. What kind of life is that? In the end, my mother, *allah yirchama*, went to the housing office and banged her fist on the table, and after a lot of screaming and yelling they agreed to give us an apartment in Lod. Provided, that is, we gave them a deposit of three hundred *lirot*."

"Three hundred *lirot*?" Victor gasped. "That was a fortune back then! Did you have it?"

"No," Farida said. "But there was this boy, a friend of Eddie's, the one who had hidden in our house. He lived in a settlement near Ramle, and when Eddie asked him to lend us the money, he agreed immediately. He said he would do anything for our family, because we had saved his life. He promised to get the money and bring it to the camp by bicycle. All the money, he said, in cash. Thanks to him we got our apartment in Lod."

"Anyway," Farida continued, engrossed in her narrative, "they were good friends, this boy and Eddie. They used to get together, either at our house or at his *moshav*, his settlement. One night Eddie biked to this boy's house, and he didn't come home. It wasn't like him to stay out without letting us know. In the middle of the night, we all went searching for him. We even called the police. Some Arab shepherds found him the next morning, lying in the road, dead. He'd fallen off his bicycle and injured himself on a boulder, and that was it. No more Eddie." Farida sighed, and a heavy silence fell.

"I'm sorry to hear that," Victor said finally. "*Walla,* I'm so sorry."

"What a life," Farida said, wiping away her tears. "One minute someone's there, the next minute he's gone. God gives and God takes, what can you do? Everything is in God's hands."

"It's really true everything is in God's hands," Victor agreed.

"You ask me what kind of life I had?" Farida's voice was bitter. "A hard life. After Eddie was gone, all my dreams were gone, too. I didn't care about anything; living and dying were the same to me. But in the end, I got married, and I had two children, and I raised them like royalty. I gave them everything. *Everything.* I shielded them from this cruel world. I looked after my husband for many years, and then he died, too. And I'm still here!" She blew her nose. "You're probably wondering, how could I have married after Eddie died? Well," she said, not waiting for an answer, "I'll tell you. One day, Moshe came to our house, and he told my mother he wanted me, and I said okay, whatever, and I married him. I would have married a donkey if it had asked me. I was lucky Moshe was a good man, and that he loved me, but things didn't go well for us. During the Yom Kippur War, he became what they call shell-shocked, and after that our life was a nightmare. He would jump out of bed in the middle of the night; convinced people were trying to kill him. Then he got sick and died, left me alone, and that was that. So now,

I'm telling you that, yes, I lived my life, but that's all it was. Nothing extraordinary."

Victor had listened to Farida's story patiently and without interruption. For a moment he thought that if he had been standing next to her he would have taken her hand and told her that her luck was about to change: he was alone, and she was alone, and why shouldn't they be together? He was a good person, and she was a good person, and the family she came from well, that was really something. When they hung up the phone, they both felt they knew each other better. They didn't talk about the future. They didn't even talk about meeting each other. But they both felt a certain intimacy that hadn't been there before.

Chapter Forty-One: Violet

Monday, May 11, 1987

It's been a month since I last wrote. It seems to me that my health is not improving; on the contrary, every treatment leaves me feeling weaker. My last few blood tests were not good. Every time I go to the hospital, they send me home without chemotherapy. I don't bother to ask questions anymore; I don't want to hear their evasive answers. The pain is unbearable; there are days when I can't sleep at all; I don't have the strength to get out of bed. It is only when the children come home that I muster the energy to rouse myself and greet them. Dan is in charge of running the household, and my wonderful sisters Farida and Chabiba are making sure we have a constant supply of food. When Noa comes home on leave, they go out of their way to make her favorite foods. Right now I have only one goal, and I am focusing on it: this diary that I am writing for you, my children. When I am awake I feel around for the thick notebook; the pen is attached to the book. I must keep writing, keep telling my story.

Eddie came to the kibbutz and loaded our meager possessions onto his friend's truck. Again, parting. I thought to myself, I have already parted from Chanan; I hadn't seen him since that wretched picnic two days earlier. I have parted from my friends; I have parted from Miriam; and I have parted from the sights, smells, and sounds: the rocky landscape, the pine trees, the roads, the smell of the stable, the clatter of silverware in the dining hall. As our truck rumbled away from the kibbutz, I felt like I was leaving one of my limbs behind. I had nothing left. Eddie sensed my sadness and tried to lift my spirits. Farida seemed happy, but all I wanted was to be left alone. In the end, he directed his rambling toward my sister.

The settlement camp was waiting for us in all its glory. Rows and rows of crowded, dirty, noisy tents. *Ima* had tried her best to make our tent nice and tidy, despite its lack of conveniences. Early the next morning, Farida and I went to look for work, and for the two years that followed, we took any kind of job we could find. We worked wherever we were needed: we did laundry at the hospital; we cleaned; we even worked at a chocolate factory. We didn't get a proper apartment despite all the promises, and after work we helped *Ima* with cleaning, with laundry, and any other chore she requested.

Aba was barely able to scrape together a living. *Ima*, clearly in charge of the whole operation, growled about her bitter fate, about the fact that *Aba* brought her to this difficult land and this pathetic tent. She directed most of her rage at *Aba*. As I wrote earlier, as soon as she landed in Israel she turned her back on him and would no longer share a bed with him. He disgusted her, with his shabby clothes, his pathetic attempts at work, his failure to support the lifestyle to which she was accustomed. She mocked him, and she encouraged all of us his children and grandchildren to mock him, too. When *Aba* expressed an opinion about something, *Ima* made him look weak, foolish, irresponsible. She cast herself as the head of the family and took it upon herself to fight for an apartment. We stood behind her, rejecting *Aba*. To this day I regret it, and I am embarrassed by my behavior. I am especially sorry that I never had a chance to ask his forgiveness. *Aba* was always in a good mood, and he never complained. He didn't ask anything of us. He adhered to his principles and his tradition and observed the *mitzvot* until his dying day. We tried to erase our foreignness, our Iraqi origins; we even learned songs in Yiddish. It was much more acceptable than singing the songs of Leila Mauraud or Farid al-Atrash.

In the end, we did get an apartment, thanks to *Ima's* persistence, Eddie's history, and Eddie's Kurdish-Iraqi friend who had hidden in our house while waiting to escape to Israel. This young man never forgot the risks we took on his behalf. Had they found him in our house, we would all have been taken directly to the town square and hanged. He lent us three hundred *lirot*, which in those days was a lot. Without that money, we would never have been able to secure the apartment in Lod.

When it was time to move, we were overjoyed. Finally, a real home to protect the family from the ravages of both winter and summer. A home of our own. But the joy was short-lived. Eddie, our pride and joy, died unexpectedly, and darkness descended over our lives. Farida was inconsolable. She never said a word to me, but in my heart I know that to this day, she hasn't recovered from his death. As for Chabiba and Yaakov, my sister and brother-in-law, their lives lost all meaning. The loss of their oldest son created a huge gap between them. Sadness filled our hearts, slammed our doors, and marked our past like a tombstone. Eddie's name was rarely spoken, but his specter haunted every family gathering, every Shabbat dinner, every wedding, every birth. Brilliant, handsome, wonderful Eddie, who had been dealt such a cruel hand. We never got over Eddie's loss, and we never will. And you, my children, it is your loss that you never knew him. I hope that through these stories, he will be a present in your lives, too. He never had a chance to have a family, and there is nobody to carry on his name. For me, Eddie is there in Guy's smile, in Farida's son, Oren, with the dimple on his chin. He is there at every family event, and every so often, my siblings and I look at each other and know that we are all feeling the same thing: the pain of Eddie's absence.

Chapter Forty-Two: Noa

Friday, October 15, 1993

Dear Aba'le,

How are you? The photos you sent me in your last letter from Oregon made me very happy. Hiking does you good. You look tanned and relaxed, and why not? If I were at a beautiful, magical place like Crater Lake, with its crystal-clear water, I'd be smiling, too. Your plan to continue south to the Mexican border sounds like a dream come true. Someday I hope to follow in your footsteps and make my way down America's west coast, but in the meantime I'm working hard. The semester started yesterday, and it looks very challenging. I'm trying to work more hours, too; I need the money. Other than that, everything here is fine. Except for the horrible suicide attacks on the buses, of course. I'm using your car, like I promised, and even though driving through the city is impossible, and parking is a nightmare, I never take the bus anymore.

You asked if I've finished my thesis on Yona Wallach. The answer is yes, I finished it, but as soon as I was done I felt like there was so much more to explore. Her curiosity, her need to dig below the surface, to expose layer after layer until she unearthed the truth—they've bewitched me. It must have taken so much courage and an extraordinary amount of creativity. I have no doubt she lived before her time. I have a hunch that one day I will return to her work and explore it further.

You also asked about *Ima*'s journal, if it's too painful for me to read, if Guy has read it yet. The answer to your second question is yes: I gave Guy the journal last week. I confess, it was hard to hand it over, but Guy also deserves to read it, and I am eager to hear his thoughts. As to your first question . . . well, it's complicated. Until now, I wasn't ready to discuss the journal with you. I couldn't get over the feeling that you had betrayed me. For a long time, I couldn't distinguish between what I was feeling and what I was thinking. Rationally, I understood that you and Aunt Farida had only the best of intentions, you weren't planning on keeping the journal from me forever, but deep inside I felt deceived. I wondered what other tricks you had up your sleeve. I kept asking myself: who gave you the right to keep something so precious to yourself, especially something *Ima* had written explicitly for me and Guy? The more I read, though, the more I understood your decision, which must not have been an easy one to make. It's not like *Ima* had written us personal messages; she wrote about her past. She wasn't trying to convey any instructions or moral admonitions, only her love for us. Still, I did learn some important lessons from her journal. I had to read it numerous times before I could decipher these lessons. I'm not sure I would have understood all the nuances had I read it earlier.

The very fact that *Ima* wrote a journal just for us never ceases to move me. I learned a lot this summer about *Ima* and the family, and, to be perfectly honest, about myself as well. *Ima* was a very strong person. She knew what it was like to immigrate to another country, and she knew about loss. From a very young age, she had to support her family and at the same time see to her own future. I also experienced loss at a young age, but my life was much easier than hers. I can learn a great deal from *Ima*, even if she's not here next to me, and this learning makes me stronger. *Ima* didn't say it explicitly, but I think I can speak for her: in our family, the women are strong. Chabiba, Farida, *Savta*, and *Ima*, and even me, know what it means to face hardship. And maybe, like Yona Wallach, we also seek the truth—and aren't afraid to face it.

My darling *Aba*, I miss you so much. Your trip abroad has also taught me something about myself, something I hadn't known before. Wherever you are, wherever *Ima* is, wherever Guy is, I am there, too. We are a unit; we are a family. The powerful connection between us fortifies me. I know that I am a part of your life, just as you are a part of mine, and the same goes for *Ima* and Guy. I know it's going to be alright.

Much love,

Noa

Chapter Forty-Three: Dan

June 15, 1987

Violet, the love of my life, passed away on Shavuot, the seventh day of the Jewish month of Sivan, June 1987, in Ichilov Hospital in Tel Aviv. She didn't have a chance to say goodbye to anyone; her body simply shut down in the middle of one of her treatments. She fell into a coma and never woke up. We called Noa and told her to come home immediately. Guy was there right away, and all of us crowded into the room. You will always be missed, my dear. May you rest in peace.

July 2, 1987

My heart is broken. I long for you so much, my soulmate. There are so many things you'll never be able to do, Violet, mother of my children. You will never be able to walk your children down the aisle. Or see your grandchildren. Never again will you hold my hand, and we won't grow old together. You didn't have the chance to write everything in your journal: how you managed to go to university despite having to work so hard to support your family and pay tuition. You did it all by yourself. You didn't write about your academic success, about how we met in the library, and how we fell in love. I am filling in those blanks, adding them to your uncompleted journal—for your sake and for the sake of our children. I am telling Noa and Guy how lucky they were to have you for a mother, what a privilege it was for me to be your partner. When we have grandchildren, I will tell them all about the grandmother they never met. I love you today as much as I loved you when I first laid eyes on you, as much as I loved you through all our years together. You are in my heart. You always will be.

January 21, 1988

Noa completed her army service today. She is talking about taking a trip to Europe, but she doesn't have any definite plans. Time passes, and we miss you so much.

March 3, 1988

Five days ago, Guy was drafted. He's in basic training, and will be serving in Intelligence.

June 4, 1988

I've been without you for an entire year, and every day feels like an eternity.

February 2, 1989

Guy has begun an officer's training course. Noa and I are so proud of him, and you would be, too, if you were here.

June 15, 1989

Two years without you. We went to the cemetery today. Your grave is cold and impersonal, and you are nowhere to be found.

May 2, 1990

Noa is back from abroad, and she's decided to live at home. I'm pleased with her decision.

June 4, 1990

Three years without you, my love. I can't believe that three years have already passed. I long for you terribly.

February 1, 1991

I decided to go back to school; I'm now working part-time. I took classes in geography and Jewish philosophy. Simply amazing. Noa decided to go to university. She starts in October.

May 15, 1991

Noa's moved out and is renting an apartment. Guy is serving in the army, stationed at a base near Tsfat. I barely see him. It's so sad without you. So empty . . .

June 4, 1991

Four years without you. I put roses on your grave. The summer is so hot, and you are not here. Noa decided to study Hebrew literature. Guy is still in the army.

March 15, 1992

Guy finished his army service and is looking for work as a waiter. For now, he's living with me until further notice. Noa finished her first semester with excellent grades; apparently she takes after her mother.

June 4, 1992

Five years, and you are not here. Sometimes I dream about you and you are so real, then I wake to another day without you. It's hard for me.

December 31, 1992

Everyone is going out for New Year's Eve, and I'm thinking about you. Without you, I'm not in the mood to celebrate.

June 4, 1993

Six whole years without you, my love. I've gotten used to your absence, but not a day goes by when I don't think about you. Noa's already finished her second year of school, and Guy has enrolled at the "Technion Institute of Technology". He left home a few months ago, and once again I am living in an empty house, without you. Each day, the pain is fresh. I've decided to take a trip to Seattle: a change of scenery, a chance to hike. It won't be the same without you. I am entrusting Farida with the journal in my absence. (Even when I'm here, she occasionally asks to borrow it, and I lend it to her until I miss it so much and ask for it back.)

I am thinking about when to let our children read your journal. I have a feeling the right time is fast approaching. They are adults now. I am waiting for a sign, a signal that they are ready for it; then I will know the time has come. I want the journal to serve its purpose.

Chapter Forty-Four: Noa

The pen slipped from Noa's hand and fell to the ground. She picked it up, rested it on the folded letter, and contemplated the sea. If there was anywhere in the world where Noa could let her emotions run wild, she thought, this was it. She focused on the horizon, and formed a picture in her mind: a father, a mother, a girl, and a boy sitting on the beach. Noa and Guy building a sand castle, *Ima* helping to build a wall, *Aba* giving out slices of cold watermelon. Soon the ice cream man would come with his popsicles, calling out, "Ice cream, ice cream, makes you fat, makes you thin, good for your body, good for your skin . . ." Every summer the same vendor, the same jingle. Every summer they'd look at each other and laugh; every summer they'd buy his popsicles. Noa looked down at the letter. She read it over, then read it again. There was more that she wanted to tell her father, to ask him about, but how could she? He was so far away.

It was only yesterday that Ofir had left for reserve duty, and she missed him already. When she looked at the water she couldn't help but think of his eyes. The apartment felt empty without him, and, as she had often done before, she escaped to the café across from the beach. At this early hour, she was the only customer. The sound of the waves mingled with the clinking of the dishes, which mingled with the noise of the congested streets. Everyone was rushing off somewhere, but there was no place Noa had to be. She sat in the corner and sipped her coffee slowly. The ice cream man didn't come here anymore; maybe, she thought, he had gone into a different business. She tried to concentrate, but it was difficult. Random thoughts kept popping into her head: her tenth or eleventh birthday party; her mother's embrace when she came home from the army; Farida heaping food onto her plate in her small apartment; Ofir admiring the new dress she was modeling. There was nothing better, she decided, than letting your imagination take you to all kinds of secret places. She felt a relief that was almost dizzying. The distress that had been gathering inside her for the last few weeks seemed to be dissipating.

She smiled to herself. When she opened her purse to pay, she came across a scrap of paper with Ehud's phone number scribbled on it. She'd had it for so long, it was practically an antique. She remembered the thrill she had felt the night of the reunion, how she had hoped to get to the heart of things. She also remembered how Ehud tightened up when he sensed her trying to shift their conversation to something more personal. His excuses bordered on ridiculous. That evening Noa understood that intimacy scared Ehud. The mysterious halo that had surrounded him all those years, that had enchanted her so much, disappeared, and he suddenly struck her as foolish, and a bit childish. When she'd come home, she'd knew that she'd never yearn for him again. And now, in the café, Noa looked at the familiar handwriting, ripped up the note, and threw the scraps into the ashtray. She paid for her coffee, and left.

2002-2006

Zichron Yaakov, Israel, and Seattle

a b
alright is okay in written dialogue—in all other instances,
   it should be *all right*
Baghdadi (using this as an adjective that can describe
   objects as well as people; e.g.,
Baghdadi man or *Baghdadi night*)

c d

e f g

h i
Holy Land

j k l
kabbalistic (adj.)

m n
menorah
makeup

o p
okay (rather than *OK* or *O.K.*)
Pesach (Passover)
phylactery (a receptacle containing a holy relic; *Judaism:*
   two black, leather cubes
containing scripture-inscribed parchment, worn on the
   left arm and forehead
during prayer)

q r

Rosh Hashanah (Jewish high holy day that marks the
    beginning of the Jewish New Year)

s t
Silon (Israeli cigarette brand)
tefellin (a religious ceremony involving phylacteries)
toward (rather than *towards*)

u v w x y z
worshiped (one "p")

punctuation / ligatures
series comma
colons (follow Garner, Chicago)
a.m. and *p.m.*, as opposed to *A.M.* or *AM* etc.
each other for two people, *one another* for more than two
    (e.g., The couple held each
    other. The coach was full, and the passengers eyed
    one another.)

names — persons
Chapter One: Violet Rosen
Violet Twaina Rosen
Aba (Violet's Father)
Naima (Violet's best friend)
Mrs. Chanukah (school administrator?)
Mrs. Zbeida (Violet's teacher)
Eddie (Violet's nephew?)
Farida (Violet's younger sister)
Violet's mother (mentioned but not by name—Georgia
    (ch. 2))

Chapter Two: Farida Sasson (youngest daughter)

Aba (Farida's and Violet's father)
Georgia (Farida's mother)
Ima (Violet's and Farida's mother)
Violet (Farida's sister; next youngest)
Farcha (Farida's sister; she and Sammy have 3 children)
Sammy (Farcha's husband)
Anwar (Farida's brother; he and Yasmin have 3 children)
Yasmin (Anwar's wife)
Habiba (Farida's sister; she and Yaakov have 5 children)
Yaakov (Habiba's husband)
Edward ((Eddie) Habiba and Yaakov's oldest son?)

Chapter Three: Noa Rosen
Noa Rosen (Violet's daughter)
Guy (Noa's brother; (Violet's son?))
Ima = "mom" in Hebrew
Aunt Farida (Violet's sister)
Aba (Farida's and Violet's father)

Chapter Four: At Aunt Farida's
  Noa
  Aunt Farida
  Sigali (Farida's son or daughter?)
  Ruthie (Sigali's daughter?)
  Shai (Sigali's son?)
  Oren (?)
  Barak (Noa's ex-boyfriend)
  Yaron (Shai's teacher?)
  Guy (Noa's brother)
  Dan (Noa's father?)

Chapter Five: Farida
  Farida (Violet's sister; Noa's aunt)
  Violet (Farida's sister; Noa's mother)

269

Noa (Violet's daughter)
Dan (Violet's husband; Noa's dad)
Eddie (Farida and Violet's nephew)
Moshe (Farida's husband)

Chapter Six: Violet
Violet
Eddie
Aunt Madeline (Violet and Farida's paternal aunt)
Violet's mom (Gorjiya)
Violet's dad (Jacob (or Yaacov))
Violet's grandmother (maternal or paternal?)
Violet's grandfather (maternal or paternal?)
Reuven

Chapter Seven: Farida
Farida
Sigal (Farida's daughter)
Ruthie (Sigal's daughter)
Shai (Sigal's son)
Violet
Eddie
Grandmother Habiba (Eddie's mom; Violet and
Farida's sister)
Farcha (Farida's sister)
Samira (Farida's grandmother)
Aunt Madeline
Leila Mourad (famous singer, mentioned in passing)
Abd al-Wahhab (another famous singer, mentioned
in passing)

Chapter Eight: The Bar Mitzvah
Violet
Violet's Grandmother

Eddie
Richie (Eddie's best friend)
Mr. and Mrs. Hardy (Richie's parents; Mr. Hardy:
manager of the Dept. of Water
and Agriculture)
Farida
Habiba (Violet's and Farida's sister)
Chacham Sasson (rabbi)

Chapter Nine: Noa
  Noa
  Ofir (Noa's roommate)
  Ehud

Chapter Ten: Violet
  Violet
  Samira (Violet's maternal grandmother)

Chapter Eleven: Noa
  Noa
  Dan Rosen (Noa's father)
  Guy (Noa's brother, mentioned by name)

Chapter Twelve: Violet
  Violet
  Anwar and his wife, Yasmin
  Violet's parents (Gorjiya and Yaakov)
  Farcha
  Habiba
  Eddie
  Yosi (Habiba's son)

Chapter Thirteen: Farida
  Farida

Dora (Farida's Romanian neighbor of 30 years)
Carmella (first floor neighbor)
Jamil (market worker)
Sigal
Shimon (hairdresser)

Chapter Fourteen: Violet
Violet
Farida
Violet's father
Various other relatives

Chapter Fifteen: Noa
Noa
Dan
Ofir

Chapter Sixteen: Violet
Violet
Farida
Aba
Anwar
Farcha
Ima
Eddie
Chabiba

Chapter Seventeen: Noa
Noa
Ehud
Avram (market proprietor)
Offir

Chapter Eighteen: Farida
Farida

Chapter Nineteen: Violet
Violet
Farida
Miriam (kibbutz mother)

Chapter Twenty: Noa
Noa
Offir

Chapter Twenty-One: Violet
Violet
Eddie
Ima
Grandma Daisy
Evelyn (non-Jewish servant)
Chabiba

Chapter Twenty-Two: Farida
Farida
Sigal (Sigi)
Ruthie (called "Tutti" by Farida)

Chapter Twenty-Three: Violet
Violet
Danny
Guy
Noa
Ima (Gorjiya, Violet's mom)
Eddie
Evelyn (*Ima's* Iraqi servant)

Chapter Twenty-Four: Noa
Noa

Chapter Thirty: Violet
Violet

Chapter Thirty-One: Noa
Noa
Violet

Chapter Thirty-Two: Violet
Violet
Eddie
Ima (Violet's mom)

Chapter Thirty-Three: Noa
Farida
Noa
Oren (and his wife and children)
Sigali

Chapter Thirty-Four: Violet
Violet
Farida
Ima
Aba
Eddie
Chanan (Violet's boyfriend)

Chapter Thirty-Five: Farida
Farida
Victor Cohen
various family members of Farida's, mentioned
during the phone conversation

Chapter Thirty-Six: Noa
Noa

Aba

Chapter Thirty-Seven: Violet
Violet

Chapter Thirty-Eight: Violet
Violet
Farida
Eddie
Ima
Chanan

Chapter Thirty-Nine: Noa
Noa
Violet
Ehud
Ofir

Chapter Forty: Farida
Farida
Dora
various family members mentioned in passing
Victor Cohen
Eddie

Chapter Forty-One: Violet
Violet
Dan
Farida
Chabiba
Eddie
Chanan
Aba
Ima
Yaakov

Chapter Forty-Two: Noa
  Noa
  Dan (her dad)
  Violet
  various family members mentioned in passing

Chapter Forty-Three: Dan
  Dan
  Violet

Chapter Forty-Four: Noa
  Noa
  Ehud
  Ofir

numbers / sections

Chapter One: Violet Rosen (first person, Violet's point of
  view)
  Monday, October 15, 1986
    Baghdad 1940

Chapter Two: Farida Sasson (third person, Farida's POV)

Chapter Three: Noa Rosen (third person, Noa's and
  Violet's POV)

Chapter Four: At Aunt Farida's (third person, Noa's POV)

Chapter Five: Farida (third person, Farida's POV)

Chapter Six: Violet (first person, Violet's POV)
  Wednesday, October 17, 1986

Chpater Seven: Farida (third person, Farida's POV)

Chapter Eight: The Bar Mitzvah (first person, Violet's POV)
Thursday, October 18, 1986

Chapter Nine: Noa (third person, Noa's POV)
Friday, January 20, 1987

Chapter Ten: Violet (first person, Violet's POV)

Chapter Eleven: Noa (third person, Noa's and Dan's POV)

Chapter Twelve: Violet (first person, Violet's POV)
Sunday, January 22, 1987

Chapter Thirteen: Farida (third person, Farida's POV)

Chapter Fourteen: Violet (first person, Violet's POV)
Wednesday, February 11, 1987

Chapter Fifteen: Noa (third person; Noa and Ofir's POV)

Chapter Sixteen: Violet (first person, Violet's POV)
Sunday, February 15, 1987

Chapter Seventeen: Noa (third person, Noa's POV)

Chapter Eighteen: Farida (third person, Farida's POV)

Chapter Nineteen: Violet (first person, Violet's POV)
Friday, February 27, 1987

Chapter Twenty: Noa (third person, Noa's and Ofir's POV)
Monday, February 16, 1987

Chapter Twenty-One: Violet (first person, Violet's POV)
Sunday, February 17, 1987

Chapter Twenty-Two: Farida (third person, Farida's POV)

Chapter Twenty-Three: Violet (first person, Violet's POV)
Sunday, March 1, 1987

Chapter Twenty-Four: Noa (third person, Noa's POV)

Chapter Twenty-Five: Farida (third person, Farida's and Ruthie's POV)

Chapter Twenty-Six: Violet (first person, Violet's POV)
Monday, March 16, 1987

Chapter Twenty-Seven: Violet (first person, Violet's POV)
Thursday, March 26, 1987

Chapter Twenty-Eight: Noa (third person, Noa's POV)

Chapter Twenty-Nine: Farida (third person, Farida's POV)

Chapter Thirty: Violet (first person, Violet's POV)
Friday, April 3, 1987

Chapter Thirty-One: Noa (third person, Noa's POV)

Chapter Thirty-Two: Violet (first person, Violet's POV)

Chapter Thirty-Three: Noa (third person, Noa's POV)

Chapter Thirty-Four: Violet (first person, Violet's POV)

Chapter Thirty-Five: Farida (third person, Farida's POV)

Chapter Thirty-Six: Noa (third person, Noa's POV)

Chapter Thirty-Seven: Violet (first person, Violet's POV)
Tuesday, April 7, 1987

Chapter Thirty-Eight: Violet (first person, Violet's POV)
Wednesday, April 8, 1987

Chapter Thirty-Nine: Noa (third person, Noa's POV)

Chapter Forty: Farida (third person, Farida's POV)

Chapter Forty-One: Violet (first person, Violet's POV)
Monday, May 11, 1987)

Chapter Forty-Two: Noa (first person (via a letter), Noa's POV)
Friday, October 15, 1993

Chapter Forty-Three: Dan (first person (via journal entries), Dan's POV)
Various dates in 1987 and 1988

Chapter Forty-Four: Noa (third person, Noa's POV)

names — places, things
Achziv River
Baghdad

Basra
B'nei Brak (city in Israel east of Tel Aviv)
Carmel Mountains (in Israel)
Chaim Nachman Bialik (Israeli national poet)
Chara (Iraqi town)
Chidekel River (in Iraq)
Chifel (village outside of Hili)
Devorah Omer (Israeli writer, born 1932)
Eilat (Israel's southernmost city)
Farid al-Atrash (Iraqi musician)
Haman (vizier of the Persian empire; antagonist in the
    book of Esther)
Hili (city in Iraq)
Hilla
Hillel Yaffe Hospital
Kinneret (Israeli spa and hotel)
Leila Mauraud (Iraqi musician)
Lod (an Israeli city on the Sharon Plain, 9 miles southeast
    of Tel Aviv)
Nahariya (city?)
Netanya (city in Israel)
Petach Tikvah (city in Israel)
Ramat Gan (Tel Aviv suburb)
Ramle (town in Israel)
Sidney Ali Beach
Silon (Israeli cigarette brand)
Technion
Tel Aviv
Tel Hashomer
Tenuvah (Israel's main dairy)
Zichron Ya'akov (town in Israel, 35 miles south of Haifa)

caps / small caps

eras in small caps

foreign words/expressions
aba (means "dad" in Hebrew)
aba'le (diminutive form of "dad")
Aliyah ("ascent"—basic tenet of Zionist ideology)
al burian (fluently)
allah yirchama
Ana Araf
Ashkenazi (Jews of central and eastern Europe)
baba (yeast cookies)
bagrut exams
bar mitzvah (coming of age ceremony for boys)
bat mitzvah (coming of age ceremony for girls)
Bint Ruven (the daughter of Ruven?)
brit (rite of circumcision)
chai ("life" or "living")
chalri
chubiz (Iraqi bread)
finjan (coffee pot?)
gute (?)
hanachat tefillin
ima (means "mom" in Hebrew)
jazira (tiny islands)
jifa (?)
ka'kaat (small pretzel)
kibbutz
kibbutzim
krayot
kubot
lady-ot (Hebrew for "lady"?)
lirot (Israeli currency?)
ma'abara (transit camp)
ma'amul (date-filled cookies)
machbuz (Jewish/Iraqi pastries)

matanah (gift)
matateh (broom)
megillah (scroll containing the biblical narrative of the
    book of Esther)
mitzvah (a good deed)
mitzvot
mkhalela (turnips steeped in saltwater; pickles)
mlabas (a dessert)
moshav (settlement?)
Moshiac (Messiah)
nu
Pesach (passover?)
Purim (a Jewish festival celebrated on the 14th day of the
    month of Adar in
commemoration of the deliverance of the Jews in Persia
    from destruction by
Haman)
sambusak bejiben (a cheese-filled pastry)
savta (grandmother)
Shabbat (the Sabbath)
Shabbat Shalom
Sha'ar Aliyah
Shavuat (Spring holiday—knows as "Visitor's Day" in Iraq)
shehechiyanu blessing
"Shehechiyanu v'kimanu v'higianu lazman hazeh, amen."
Shevit (a large fish: turbot)
Shumash (the best school in Iraq)
tefellin ceremony
Tena Maca
tfadal
tum ajam (garlic marinated in salt and curry)
tvit (chicken with rice?)
ud (fat-bellied guitar)
ulpan

Um Anwar (mother of Anwar—what townspeople called
    Farida and Violet's
Mom; Anwar = Farida and Violet's brother; Gorjiya's
    first-born)
"*Wai li*," exclaimed Naima.
walla
"*Ya'allah*," I begged.
ya binati
Ya buya (Arabic; exclamation of woe)
ya walli
Yishayahu (Isaiah)
zangula (honey-dipped pastry)
zemirot (Jewish hymns)

ornaments / other

CPSIA information can be obtained at www.ICGtesting.com
264368BV00001B/1/P